PENGU

HERE, THERE AND EVERYWHERE

Sudha Murty is the chairperson of the Infosys Foundation and a bestselling author. She has a master's degree in electrical engineering from the Indian Institute of Science, Bengaluru. She started her career as a development engineer and has also taught computer science at Bangalore University colleges. She is a columnist for English and Kannada dailies, with twenty-nine books and 200 titles to her credit. Her books have been translated into twenty languages. Among the awards she has received are the R.K. Narayan Award for Literature, the Padma Shri in 2006, the Attimabbe Award from the Government of Karnataka for excellence in Kannada literature in 2011 and, most recently, the Lifetime Achievement Award at the Crossword Book Awards in 2018. She has received seven honorary doctorates from universities in India.

Here, There and Everywhere

Best-Loved Stories of Sudha Murty

PENGUIN BOOKS

An imprint of Penguin Random House

PENGUIN BOOKS

USA | Canada | UK | Ireland | Australia
New Zealand | India | South Africa | China

Penguin Books is part of the Penguin Random House group of companies
whose addresses can be found at global.penguinrandomhouse.com

Published by Penguin Random House India Pvt. Ltd
7th Floor, Infinity Tower C, DLF Cyber City,
Gurgaon 122 002, Haryana, India

Penguin
Random House
India

First published in Penguin Books by Penguin Random House India 2018

Copyright © Sudha Murty 2018

15 14 13

ISBN 9780143444343

Typeset in Dante MT Std by Manipal Digital Systems, Manipal
Printed at Thomson Press India Ltd, New Delhi

www.penguin.co.in

To Shini,
You are my reflection in thoughts,
in deeds and in appearance

Contents

Introduction

Often, I sense that there is a lot of myself in my stories, whether it is my friends or family or the people I meet. However, the experiences that I write about are mine. I cannot disassociate from myself while writing about them. This book contains some of my most cherished experiences that are like beautiful flowers to me and have been put together here as if to complete a garland. While most of the experiences are from previously published books, there are two new flowers: one that highlights my literary journey and the other that elaborates on the true meaning of philanthropy.

This book is dedicated to my brother Shrinivas. Writing about him is easy enough and yet so difficult. I look like him, think like him, read like him and eat like him. I have enjoyed his company since he was born—I was the second child and he was the fourth. I can spend hours with him without any boredom setting in.

Today, he is a renowned astrophysicist who has innumerable awards and distinguished accomplishments to his credit. His work is all Greek to me, just like mine is to him. I think he is extremely focused and absolutely impractical—he doesn't care much about his appearance, social appropriateness, what others think of him, or even food for that matter. I am much more practical in my approach. In my journey, I have been an integral part of the administration of many organizations. But despite what may appear to be major differences, we are the best of friends.

When Shrinivas and I were children, we had decided to memorize a dictionary each during the summer holidays. Shrinivas was part of the first batch of a recently formed English-medium school in our locality. That school was Kendriya Vidyalaya. So, he chose to learn the English dictionary while I defaulted to the one in Kannada. At that time, the children in the family had been assigned the task of walking the family dog. At times, both of us did not want to take him out individually because we wanted to use that time to learn a few more words. After some thought, we decided to walk the dog together in an effort to recite the new words we had learnt and to avoid monotony. During our walks, we did more than what we had planned. I educated myself about *madhyama* yoga that my brother was learning in Sanskrit, and I spoke to him about trigonometry. I was surprised at the speed with which he learnt its concepts despite the fact that he was younger than me and that it was not even part of his syllabus at school. Other times, we loved to debate about our difference in opinion on various topics.

From the time that I can remember, Shrinivas has loved his three sisters equally. When he was sixteen, he had gone to Nagpur for a debate and won a cash prize. With that money, he bought one sari. He brought it back and gave it to the three of us, saying, 'This is all that I could afford, and I want all of you to share this sari.'

Time has passed and our lives have changed. Still, the four of us are there for each other when things get rough and when happiness abounds.

My brother has been living in a different country for the past forty years, and we meet only annually. But we remain strongly connected and he continues to occupy a very special place in my heart. He is caring but not very expressive and lives in his bubble of science and astrophysics, along with stars, brown dwarfs, black holes and other entities. The only gift that I can really and truly give him is this book: a dear and precious part of me.

1

A Tale of Many Tales

Every person's life is a unique story. Usually, the story becomes famous only after a person receives recognition in ways that matter to the world. If you peep into what lies deep inside, it is the changes he or she has gone through—subtle changes that the world may never understand.

Most people undertake an arduous journey full of highs and lows that helps them modify and create new perspectives, thus forming a better understanding of the world and realizing the fact that real passion is much more beautiful than the pinnacle of their accomplishments. Ironically, life appears to be barren and aimless to some achievers even after they reach a big goal.

Recently, I received the Lifetime Achievement Award from Crossword Books at Mumbai's Royal Opera House. The categories were unravelled on stage one by one: fiction, non-fiction and children's, among others. The jury members gave insights into their strategies and opinions, and my mind went back to the beginning of my literary journey.

I am not a student of literature; I did not pursue a degree in the subject. But literature has always fascinated me. I belong to a family of teachers where books are treasured and I was inclined towards books at a very young age.

I grew up in a village where the medium of communication was the local language—Kannada. Mine was a Kannada-medium school. Sometimes, a makeshift theatre under a tent would showcase Kannada movies. There were barely any radio stations either. After we finally did get a radio at home, it was monitored closely by the older members of the family who limited its use to Kannada programmes only. But as kids, we all have our ways. When the elders weren't at home, I would listen to Radio Ceylon and one of its popular shows called *Binaca Geetmala*. I even recall Sri Lanka's national anthem, *Namo Namo Mata*, which often played on that station. Other than that, there was no trace of English in my childhood but there was plenty of time to figure out my creative outlets.

My family frequently went for small day trips: temple visits, wedding-related events, picnics or a visit to a historical site.

As soon as we would return home and settle for the evening, my mother would insist, 'Now sit and write about your day. You may not remember tomorrow what you have seen today, and writing is a wonderful exercise for your tiny fingers and young minds.'

I almost always resisted her instructions. Sitting in one place after an exciting day didn't sound like a lot of fun. So, I would respond, 'I will write tomorrow.'

'That's fine. You can also have your dinner tomorrow then,' my mother would say.

This is how I was forced to sit and write.

Once I began writing, I slowly but surely began to find it fun. I could play with combinations of the fifty-two letters in the Kannada alphabet and create meaningful words to express my feelings: joy, sadness, excitement and anything else that I felt. Before long, writing became a fond habit.

For many, many years, I wrote down my daily thoughts—at least twenty-five lines a day for two decades, not realizing that the process was inadvertently improving my expression and adding clarity to my ideas. For this, I owe gratitude to my first teacher, my mother.

As a teenager, I began writing with a tinge of seriousness, a lot of adventure and perhaps even a shade of romance. Modernity was the best thing there was, or so I thought.

I wrote about Mozart and submitted the article to a local newspaper. When it appeared on a Sunday, I was ecstatic. I took the newspaper to school and shared the article with my teachers and classmates. My friends looked at me with awe and I felt like I had really achieved something! It was very rare for women to get published in those days and, in that instant, I realized that I was possibly the only girl in school whose article had been picked up by a newspaper.

Later, I wrote a romantic story and sent it to the same newspaper. Days passed but I did not receive a reply. So, I sent a reminder to the editor with a prepaid stamped envelope, hoping that it would encourage him to reply. Still, there was nothing. Finally, I gathered all the courage that I could muster and went to meet the editor. As expected, it was a man since women editors and journalists were absolutely unheard of then. The editor looked at me and spoke gently, 'My child, we cannot publish this article. A good piece of literature must use the right mix of reality and imagination. Experience, observation, introspection: these senses must be developed consciously. So don't give up, but think about the feedback that I have given you today.'

As I sat and brooded over this, I understood that imagination in itself was only a shining thread and not a piece of beautiful cloth, that writing simply about facts or real issues could be dry and writing without creativity would be akin to reporting. The editor was right—a good mix of both aspects makes for interesting and impactful writing. It was a lesson that I have never forgotten and one that I practise even today!

My mother encouraged me. She said, 'Don't worry about getting published. Even if you don't, don't stop writing. I can promise you that when you look back and read your articles again after ten years, you will see the improvement in your expression.'

Motivated, I kept writing.

Later, when I submitted my articles to a local newspaper, some of them began to be published occasionally—like a pleasant shower during the summer. There was no financial compensation for these articles, and I didn't expect any either. Getting my writing published felt like the biggest compensation!

The years flew by. I completed the tenth grade from my Kannada-medium school and joined an English-medium college.

In the old days, nobody cared about the plight of the teenagers who were switching from Kannada to English as a medium of instruction. There were many like me in the same rocky boat. To make it worse, it was the critical year where my academic performance would become the greatest factor in deciding whether I got admission to engineering or medical courses or not. Some of my peers were so aghast at the change in language that they changed their courses to study the arts—not because they really wanted to change their subjects, but because science was known to be tough and the arts course was thought to be easy, giving them a chance to do well while accommodating the change in language.

I was fifteen years old then and unable to write a single paragraph in English. Confused, I approached my mother. She said, 'You love Kannada and writing in it, don't you?'

I nodded.

'Then don't get scared now. English is just another language. You simply have to read more in English and start writing in it too until you get comfortable with the language.'

From that day on, I concentrated on reading English books and found it very challenging. But I persevered, unwilling to give up, and wrote at least one paragraph in English every day. My grandfather gifted me an English–Kannada dictionary for my birthday that year, which became my constant companion for years after that.

Luckily for me, mathematics, physics and chemistry do not require extensive English. I managed to do well and get admission to an engineering college. For a brief period, I stopped writing because of my schedule. Apart from the regular coursework, the engineering drawings were tough and the experiments tedious. Not to mention that I had to manage everything alone. There was barely any time to write.

The years flew by and I wrote less and less, but I read more and more. My inclination towards reading was augmented by my husband's love for it. Since the day we met, he has been gifting me books and continues to do so even today. There is always a brief message on the first page of each gift: 'To You, From Me'. We read some books together, especially biographies and humour. But I was also interested in other subjects such as history, technology and anthropology while Murthy was more motivated towards reading about communism and coding.

There was an inherent shortage of money but the desire to read more books remained as strong as ever. So, Murthy and I decided to set aside a budget of three hundred rupees a month to purchase books from the once-iconic Strand Book Stall. That was all that we could afford back then, and we would save this money by cutting down on expenses in other areas—we would travel only in crowded buses and local trains and cook and clean at home. That helped us save the money we needed for the books. But even then, this budget wasn't enough for me. During those days, shopkeepers would frown at customers who spent a lot of time simply browsing through books. 'Please don't touch the books if you don't intend to buy them because then they will start looking used and old and a potential customer will not want to buy them,' they would say. So, I would stand at a distance and stare at the books with greedy eyes.

In 1979, I had very little money but a lot of spirit. So, off I went to America all alone with a backpack. One late evening in New York, two policemen flagged me down suspecting that I was carrying drugs in my obviously heavy bag. When they scanned my bag, all they found was what I was truly addicted to—curd rice! They were so surprised at their finding that I had to explain where I was from and the significance of curd rice in south India.

Many more of such daring incidents marked my journey. When I came back to India, I wrote about my adventures in Kannada, titled my writing 'From beyond the Atlantic', and kept it aside. The thought of publishing it never crossed my mind.

More than a year later, I was speaking to my father about my adventures and my writing when he suggested, 'Why don't you go ahead and publish this as a book? You already know how rare it is for young girls from our area to go backpacking to an unknown land. It is sure to be a unique book for that reason alone.'

I wasn't prepared for that thought. Me: an author? When I thought of the word, I was usually reminded of people like Jerome K. Jerome, P.G. Wodehouse, V.S. Naipaul, Jean-Paul Sartre and Kannada writers such as Triveni and Bhyrappa. An author must be of that calibre, or so I thought. I felt silly and strange just at the thought that someone as ordinary as me was thinking of becoming an author.

I brooded over it for a few days until the feeling settled. Then I wondered: 'Is there anything wrong in sending my manuscript to a publisher? The worst that could happen is that they would reject my work. But I am used to rejection, am I not?'

With bravado in my heart, I approached a popular Kannada publishing house called Manohara Grantha Mala, whose legendary founder G.B. Joshi was known for giving newcomers a break. Among the authors who had started out this way were Girish Karnad and M.K. Indira. I spoke hesitantly to Mr Joshi and gave him my manuscript, who said that he would contact me within two days. Forty-eight hours later, I was impatient and tense. My feelings at that time were somewhat similar to going through labour during a pregnancy. Finally, he informed me that he would publish my manuscript. He never spoke of royalty and I did not ask for it. That day, my family and I celebrated as if I had become a prominent author already. Nevertheless, it was a first. I was the first author in my family of seventy-five first and second cousins, aunts and uncles.

Much like a pregnancy, the book took ten months to reach the market. When I heard of this development, I took a bus from Hubli to Dharwad to accept my first brainchild from the publisher and received the first twenty copies with great affection. I was thrilled!

I wondered how I would distribute these copies among my big family. In the end, I gave a few copies to my parents-in-law, a few more to my friends and kept three with myself. The remaining copies were exhausted quickly. Some friends congratulated me and brought boxes of sweets. Others said with pride, 'We had no clue that an engineer could turn into a writer too! We are very happy!' A few remarked, 'Even we would have written a book had we gone to America and returned. You need money to travel and write a book.'

The first book finally gave me the title of being an author and made me want more.

In 1979, when I was in Jamshedpur, then in Bihar, for two months, I found myself all alone in the company guest house. It was then that I conceived the idea for my next book. I came from a middle-class background and was quite fascinated by how rich women led their lives, especially those whose husbands were perpetually busy with business. I decided to use this fascination and some of my imagination for this novel.

I returned to Mumbai with the idea still lingering in my mind. When I ran the idea past Mr Murthy, he gave me a blank stare. 'I can't help you there, I'm afraid. I am neither rich nor am I a lady.'

So, that was that. After some thought, I made some inquiries with various colleagues at work and observed the 'rich' women that I could see on Juhu beach, in tow with their children and ayahs.

The result of the imagination and research led to my first novel, *Athirikthe*, in Kannada. As I wrote it, I allowed myself to enter the lead character's mind and feel the joy and pain of her circumstances. At the end, I had to make an effort to exit from the character's life and return to my own. Thus began my journey in Kannada literature. This time, I went through another publisher who was located in Mysore.

I continued to write. My subsequent novels, however, were rejected. I figured that if I wanted to grab more eyeballs, I must try my hand at writing a series for a newspaper. To my surprise, even these were rejected. Some papers did not respond at all while others said that my writing wasn't series material.

Years passed, and I continued to read avidly.

One day, I went to a wedding where I saw a young girl with leucoderma sitting in front of me, having a meal. Just then, someone from the family came and said to her, 'You cannot sit here with the others. You have leucoderma. Please get up.'

Humiliated, the girl cried and left immediately.

This behaviour hurt me. I am the daughter of a doctor and I know that unlike leprosy, leucoderma is only a cosmetic disease. It is not contagious and not proven to be hereditary either. Then why do people behave this way with fellow beings?

The incident provoked me into undertaking some research. As I spoke to people, I realized that many engagements were broken and marriages called off, especially in cases where one or more of the bride's relatives had the disease but she did not. I had long chats with dermatologists and rebelled strongly against this heinous treatment which does nothing but kill confidence.

For the first time in my life, I thought of writing about this to create awareness, but in the form of a story. This is how my novel *Mahashweta* was born.

Many, many years later, I was at another wedding. To my pleasant surprise, the groom came up to me and said, 'I have read *Mahashweta* and today I am marrying a girl who has leucoderma. The book completely changed my perspective.'

It was the day that I realized that perhaps I could make a difference if I continued to write about issues I was passionate about.

In the seventies and the eighties, going to America was an outstanding achievement. India wasn't close to liberalization yet and the number of job opportunities was very low in the country. The American dollar, however, was a magic wand—one dollar equalled ten rupees. People who settled there and came back to India for a vacation almost always looked down upon those here. Even the local families differentiated between the children and grandchildren who were in the US and those who stayed here. It was but natural that the wives and daughters who lived in America got much more attention and importance.

But I knew by then that life in America wasn't as green as it was made out to be. Living there wasn't devoid of struggles.

So, I wrote *Dollar Bahu* (or *Dollar Sose*) in Kannada. The manuscript first became a series in a newspaper, then a book and then a television series. It was even translated into Italian along with other Indian languages. Today, it is still widely available in bookshops.

My journey with Kannada continued, and the thought of writing in English didn't even cross my mind.

The year 1998 marked my very first book launch with the novel *Yashasvi*. The event was held at Mythic Society in

Bangalore. To me, it was like a small wedding signifying the marriage of my book to the publisher. I invited many people. All kith and kin fond of literature came for the launch, including some of my wonderful friends who couldn't even read Kannada. But they loved me and were proud of the fact that I was an author. One of them gifted me a silver idol of Saraswati, the goddess and symbol of knowledge. For the first time, and what I thought may also be the last, I stood on stage, spoke to my readers and expressed my love for books and Kannada. Little did I know that this would be the first of many public events.

One day, T.J.S. George, the editor of the *New Indian Express*, sent word that I should write my columns in English. He simply said, 'A language is but a vehicle. It's the person inside who's weaving the story that's more important. You are a storyteller. So, just get on with your story and the language will fall into place.'

With his kind words and encouragement, I began writing in English. My columns, named 'Episodes', started to appear in the *New Indian Express* on 12 November 2000. I was in Shimoga the day I heard someone in a hotel say, 'Sudha Murty has written a column in English.' Instantly, I was elevated to being an English writer by a stranger. It took me some time to believe that people wanted to read my columns. This journey continued with other avenues like the *Times of India*, *The Hindu* and the *Week*.

One advantage of writing in English was that it led me to form friendships with people from different states and walks of life. One of those turned out to be the late

President A.P.J. Abdul Kalam. This was 2001, and he wasn't our President yet. He was a scientist at the Defence Research and Development Organization (DRDO). He happened to read one of my columns in the *Week*, an Indian news magazine, and said that the humour in my writing was nice and the message strong. He asked how I had learnt the art of ending an article with a gist of the story and expressed interest in meeting me.

A year later, my first book in English came out as a collection of my columns thanks to George, who introduced me to East West Books Pvt. Ltd in Chennai. George, with his genuine encouragement, wrote the foreword for the book and gave it an enchanting title: *Wise and Otherwise*.

I realized that when a book is released in English, it is read by more people and translations into regional languages happen more easily. Today, my books have been translated into all major Indian languages and are read in most states of India.

As the years passed, the Infosys Foundation's work provided me with experiences that enlarged my canvas even as the writing continued. I approached many publishers who rejected my manuscripts. They said, 'Your language is too simple. It is not flowery or sophisticated and comes across as too simple and even naive. Our opinion is that people will not appreciate it.' A few suggested, 'You tell your story to someone who has a good command over the English language. They will rewrite it and, together, you both can co-author.'

But I didn't agree. I wanted to keep my style distinctive and portray it exactly the way I am.

Along the way, I realized the importance of a good editor—someone who can take the book to greater heights. I have learnt that a great editor must be a reflection of the author, someone who understands the author. I am extremely lucky to have found these qualities in my young and bright editor Shrutkeerti Khurana, who is a talented engineer and a management graduate with an immense love for the English language. I have known Shrutee since the day she was born because I was friends with her parents even then. I have seen her growing up, she has seen me getting old, and our bond has deepened with each passing day over the years. She reads my mind, tells me frankly where I am wrong, where she is getting bored with my writing and edits as required. In addition to work, we both love reading and discuss countless things—things that are here, there and everywhere.

I also want to thank my wonderful family who knew of my love for writing and understood it and allowed me to prioritize it over their needs.

In time, Penguin Random House became my sole English publisher. I was also fortunate enough to get interest from publishers who worked in regional languages, and I have remained with them since the beginning. For the Marathi language, there is Mehta Publishing House in Pune, R.R. Sheth in Ahmedabad for Gujarati, Prabhat Prakashan in Delhi for Hindi translations, DC Books in Kottayam for Malayalam and Alakananda Prachuranalu in Vijayawada for Telugu translations, among others.

One day, I received an email from a Gujarati reader who asked, 'Sudha Ben, you look like a Gujarati and you even eat like one. Your books are really wonderful. I am very curious: how did you get married to a south Indian?'

The email made me smile. I responded to the reader that I was a south Indian myself and that the quality of the translations in Gujarati was so good that she thought that I belonged to her land.

During one of my international trips, I was pleasantly surprised to come across my books in New Jersey. As I beamed and picked one of them up, the Gujarati shopkeeper looked at me and commented, 'Take it. *Saras che.*' He meant that the book was nice and that I should buy it.

Happily, I nodded.

As I heard my name being called on stage again for the Lifetime Achievement Award, my mind returned to the present and I slowly climbed the steps leading up to the stage. Each step was a reminder of the journey that has lasted over forty years. It was a journey filled with rejections, negative comments and disapprovals, along with appreciation, a lot of love and affection. I hope that I have somehow been the voice for people who remain shy, hidden, unknown and yearn for an outlet of their expression.

I have lost count of the number of times people have said to me, 'I can't write. But I want to share my story. Will you write it and share it with the world?'

Some of my students have frequently remarked, 'Madam, each of us has faltered and made mistakes during the course of our lives. We don't want the next generation to go through trying times that can be avoided with just a little bit of advice and wisdom. Will you tell our stories in your book?'

I am always hesitant. I don't want to take anyone's privacy for granted or share anything without his or her permission and faith. But powerful stories, no matter where they come from, are meant to be told. So, I fancy myself as only a carrier.

My vast experience with the truly underprivileged in India, my publishers who had unwavering faith in me, my excellent editor and my readers have made me what I am today. So, my journey is not mine alone. It is also about the people around me. There's a part of me that realizes that my writing emanates from Saraswati, the goddess of knowledge, learning and writing, and that I am only her scribe. Without her assent and blessing, I can't write even one line.

Today, I have a résumé of twenty-nine books and am a bilingual writer in both English and Kannada with writings across categories such as novels, non-fiction, fiction, children's books, travelogues and technical books. My books have been translated into twenty languages and one Braille system. This book is my 200th title. As many as 2.6 million copies of my books have been sold, of which 1.5 million are in English alone.

But I have also learnt the hard way that nothing succeeds like success. The proof, I've been told, lies in the sales and the number of reprints sold in the last decade and more. Despite the numbers, I know that I am not an author for the English elite and that I cannot spin words like the books from the West or some Indian authors. But English is no longer a language meant only for the elite, as it was in the days before.

Somehow, the common people of India have found a way to welcome English into their daily lives, and that includes me too. I can only tell stories from the heart and in a simple manner. That's all I really know, and that is also the only thing in the world that is truly mine.

2

'Amma, What Is Your Duty?'

At that time, my daughter, Akshata, was a teenager. By nature she was very sensitive. On her own, she started reading for blind children at Ramana Maharishi Academy for the Blind at Bangalore. She was a scribe too. She used to come home and tell me about the world of blind people. Later she wrote an essay on them, called 'I Saw the World through the Blind Eyes of Mary'. Mary was a student at the academy who was about to appear for the pre-university exam. Once, Akshata took Mary to Lalbagh for a change. The conversation between them was quite unusual.

'Mary, there are different types of red roses in this park,' Akshata told her.

Mary was surprised. 'Akshata, what do you mean by red?'

Akshata did not know how to explain what was red. She took a rose and a jasmine, and gave them to Mary.

'Mary, smell these two flowers in your hand. They have different smells. The first one is a rose. It is red in colour. The second one is jasmine. It is white. Mary, it is difficult to explain what is red and what is white. But I can tell you that in this world there are many colours, which can be seen and differentiated only through the eyes and not by touch. I am sorry.'

After that incident Akshata told me, 'Amma, never talk about colours when you talk to blind people. They feel frustrated. I felt so helpless when I was trying to explain to Mary. Now I always describe the world to them by describing smells and sounds which they understand easily.'

Akshata also used to help a blind boy called Anand Sharma at this school. He was the only child of a schoolteacher from Bihar. He was bright and jolly. He was about to appear for his second pre-university exam.

One day, I was heading for an examination committee meeting. At that time, I was head of the department of computer science at a local college. It was almost the end of February. Winter was slowly ending and there was a trace of summer setting in. Bangalore is blessed with beautiful weather. The many trees lining the roads were flowering and the city was swathed in different shades of violet, yellow and red.

I was busy getting ready to attend the meeting, hence I was collecting old syllabi, question papers and reference books. Akshata came upstairs to my room. She looked worried and tired. She was then studying in class ten. I thought she was tired preparing for her exams. As a mother, I have never insisted my children study too much. My parents never did that. They always believed the child has to be responsible. A responsible child will sit down to study on his or her own.

I told Akshata, 'Don't worry about the exams. Trying is in your hands. The results are not with you.' She was annoyed and irritated by my advice. 'Amma, I didn't talk about any examination. Why are you reminding me of that?'

I was surprised at her irritation. But I was also busy gathering old question papers so I did not say anything. Absently, I looked at her face. Was there a trace of sadness on it? Or was it my imagination?

'Amma, you know Anand Sharma. He came to our house once. He is a bright boy. I am confident that he will do very well in his final examination. He is also confident about it. He wants to study further.'

She stopped. By this time I had found the old question papers I had been looking for, but not the syllabus. My search was on. Akshata stood facing me and continued, 'Amma, he wants to study at St Stephen's in Delhi. He does not have anybody. He is poor. It is an expensive place. What should he do? Who will support him? I am worried.'

It was getting late for my meeting so I casually remarked, 'Akshata, why don't you support him?'

'Amma, where do I have the money to support a boy in a Delhi hostel?'

My search was still on.

'You can forfeit your birthday party and save money and sponsor him.'

At home, even now both our children do not get pocket money. Whenever they want to buy anything they ask me and I give the money. We don't have big birthday parties.

Akshata's birthday party would mean calling a few of her friends to the house and ordering food from the nearby fast-food joint, Shanthi Sagar.

'Amma, when an educated person like you, well travelled, well read and without love for money does not help poor people, then don't expect anyone else to do. Is it not your duty to give back to those unfortunate people? What are you looking for in life? Are you looking for glamour or fame? You are the daughter of a doctor, granddaughter of a schoolteacher and come from a distinguished teaching family. If you cannot help poor people then don't expect anyone else to do it.'

Her words made me abandon my search. I turned around and looked at my daughter. I saw a sensitive young girl pleading for the future of a poor blind boy. Or was she someone reminding me of my duty towards society? I had received so much from that society and country but in what way was I giving back? For a minute I was frozen. Then I realized I was holding the syllabus I was looking for in my hand and it was getting late for the meeting.

Akshata went away with anger and sadness in her eyes. I too left for college in a confused state of mind.

When I reached, I saw that as usual the meeting was delayed. Now I was all alone. I settled down in my chair in one of the lofty rooms of the college. There is a difference between loneliness and solitude. Loneliness is boring, whereas in solitude you can inspect and examine your deeds and your thoughts.

I sat and recollected what had happened that afternoon. Akshata's words were still ringing in my mind.

I was forty-five years old. What was my duty at this age? What was I looking for in life?

I did not start out in life with a lot of money. A great deal of hard work had been put in to get to where we were today. What had I learnt from the hard journey that was my life? Did I work for money, fame or glamour? No, I did not work for those; they came accidentally to me. Initially I worked for myself, excelling in studies. After that I was devoted to Infosys and my family. Should not the remaining part of my life be used to help those people who were suffering for no fault of theirs? Was that not my duty? Suddenly I remembered JRD's parting advice to me: 'Give back to society.'

I decided that was what I was going to do for the rest of my life. I felt relieved and years younger.

I firmly believe no decision should be taken emotionally. It should be taken with a cool mind and when you are aware of the consequences. After a week, I wrote my resignation letter as head of the department and opted only for a teacher's post.

I am ever grateful to Akshata for helping to bring this happiness and satisfaction to my work and life. It means more to me than the good ranks I got in school, and my wealth.

When I see hope in the eyes of a destitute person, see the warm smile on the faces of once helpless people, I feel so satisfied. They tell me that I am making a difference.

I joined the Infosys Foundation as a founder trustee. The foundation took up a number of philanthropic projects for the benefit of the poor in different states of India.

I received many awards on various occasions. One of them was the Economic Times Award given to the Infosys Foundation. As a trustee I was invited to receive this award. At that time I remembered my guru. Now she was a student in the US. I told her, 'At least for one day you must come for this award ceremony in Mumbai. If you had not woken me up at the right time, I would not have been receiving it today. I want you to be present.'

I will remain indebted to Akshata forever for the way she made me change my life and the lesson she taught me.

3

Honesty Comes from the Heart

One bright June morning three years ago, I was reading my Kannada newspaper as usual. It was the day the Secondary School Leaving Certificate results had been published. While columns of roll numbers filled the inside pages, the list of rank holders and their photographs took up almost the entire front page.

I have a great fascination for rank holders. Rank is not merely an index of one's intelligence, it also indicates the hard work and perseverance that students have put in to reach their goal. My background—I was brought up in a professor's family—and my own experience as a teacher have led me to believe this.

Of all the photographs in that morning's newspaper, one boy's snapshot caught my attention. I could not take my eyes off him. He was frail and pale, but there was an endearing sparkle in his eyes. I wanted to know more about him. I read that his name was Hanumanthappa and that he had secured the eighth rank. That was all the information I could gather.

The next day, to my surprise, his photograph was published again, this time with an interview. With growing interest I learnt that Hanumanthappa was a coolie's son, the oldest of five children. They belonged to a tribal group. He was unable to study further, he said in the interview, because he lived in a village and his father, the sole breadwinner, earned only Rs 40 a day.

I felt sorry for this bright boy. Most of us send our children to tuitions and to coaching classes, we buy them reference books and guides, and provide the best possible facilities for them without considering the cost. But it was different for Hanumanthappa of Rampura. He had excelled in spite of being denied some of the basic necessities of life.

While I was thinking about him with the newspaper still in my hands, I gazed at a mango tree in my neighbour's compound. It looked its best with a fresh bark, tender green leaves glistening with dewdrops and mangoes that were about to ripen in a few days. Beyond the tree was a small potted plant that, I noticed, had remained almost the same ever since it had been potted. It was a calm morning. The air was cool and fresh. My thoughts were running free. The continuous whistle of our pressure cooker broke the silence, reminding me that half an hour had passed.

Hanumanthappa's postal address was provided in the interview. Without wasting much time, I took a postcard and wrote to him. I wrote only two lines, saying that I was interested in meeting him and asking whether he could come to Bangalore. Just then my father, ever a practical man, returned from his morning walk. He read the postcard and said, 'Where will he have the money to come so far? If you want him to come here, send some money for his bus fare plus a little extra to buy himself a decent set of clothes.'

So I added a third line to say that I would pay for his travel and some clothes. Within four days I received a similar postcard in reply. Two sentences: in the first he thanked me for the letter, in the second he expressed his willingness to come to Bangalore and meet me. Immediately, I sent him some money and details of my office address.

When he finally arrived in our office, he looked like a frightened calf that had lost its way. It must have been his first trip to Bangalore. He was humble. He wore a clean shirt and trousers, and his hair was neatly parted and combed. The sparkle in his eyes was still there.

I got straight to the point. 'We are happy about your academic performance. Do you want to study further? We would like to sponsor you. This means we will pay your fees for any course of study you wish to take up—wherever it may be.'

He did not answer.

My senior colleague, who was in the office with me, interrupted with a smile, 'Don't go at the speed of bits and bytes. Let the boy understand what you are suggesting. He can give us his answer at the end of the day.'

When Hanumanthappa was ready to return home, he said in a low and steady tone, 'Madam, I want to pursue my studies at the Teachers' Training College in Bellary. That is the one nearest to my village.'

I agreed instantly but spoke to him a little more to find out whether there was any other course he preferred. I was trying to make it clear to him that we would pay the fees for any course he might choose. The boy, however, seemed to know exactly what he wanted.

'How much money should I send you per month? Does the college have a hostel facility?' I asked.

He said he would get back to me after collecting the correct details. Two days later, he wrote to us in his beautiful handwriting that he would require approximately Rs 300 per month. He planned to take a room on rent and share it with a friend. The two boys would cook for themselves in order to keep their expenses down.

I sent him Rs 1800 to cover his expenses for six months. He acknowledged my draft without delay and expressed his gratitude.

Time passed. One day, I suddenly remembered that I had to pay Hanumanthappa for the next six months, so I sent him another draft for Rs 1800.

This too was duly acknowledged, but I was surprised to find some currency notes in the envelope along with his letter. 'Madam,' he had written, 'it is kind of you to have sent me money for the next six months. But I was not in Bellary for the last two months. One month, our college was closed for holidays and during the next month, there was a strike. So I stayed at home for those two months. My expenditure during these months was less than Rs 300 per month. Therefore, I am sending you the Rs 300 that I have not used for the last two months. Kindly accept this amount.'

I was taken aback. Such poverty and yet such honesty. Hanumanthappa knew I expected no account of the money sent to him for his monthly expenses, yet he had made it a point to return the balance amount. Unbelievable but true!

Experience has taught me that honesty is not the mark of any particular class nor is it related to education or wealth. It cannot be taught at any university. In most people, it springs naturally from the heart.

I did not know how to react to this simple village boy's honesty. I just prayed that God would continue to bestow the best on Hanumanthappa and his family.

4

The Red Rice Granary

Every year, our country has to face natural disasters in some form. It may be an earthquake in Gujarat, floods in Orissa or a drought in Karnataka. In a poor country, these calamities cause havoc.

In the course of my work, I have found that after such calamities, many people like to donate money or materials to relief funds. We assume that most donations come from rich people, but that is not true. On the contrary, people from the middle class and the lower middle class help more. Rarely do rich people participate wholeheartedly.

A few years back, I was invited to a reputed company in Bangalore to deliver a lecture on corporate social responsibility. Giving a speech is easy. But I was not sure how many people in the audience would really understand the speech and change themselves.

After my talk was over, I met many young girls and boys. It was an affluent company and the employees were well off and well dressed. They were all very emotional after the lecture.

'Madam, we buy so many clothes every month. Can we donate our old clothes to those people who are affected by the earthquake? Can you coordinate and send these to them?'

Some of them offered other things.

'We have grown-up children, we would like to give their old toys and some vessels.'

I was very pleased at the reaction. It reminded me of the incident in the Ramayana where, during the construction of the bridge between India and Lanka, every squirrel helped Sri Rama by bringing a handful of sand.

'Please send your bags to my office. I will see that they reach the right persons.'

Within a week, my office was flooded with hundreds of bags. I was proud that my lecture had proven so effective.

One Sunday, along with my assistants, I opened the bags. What we saw left us amazed and shocked. The bags were brimming with all kinds of junk! Piles of high-heeled slippers (some of them without the pair), torn undergarments, unwashed shirts, cheap, transparent saris, toys which had neither shape nor colour, unusable bed sheets, aluminium vessels and broken cassettes were soon piled in front of us like a mountain. There were only a few good shirts, saris and usable materials. It was apparent that instead of sending the material to a garbage dump or the *kabariwala*, these people had transferred them to my office in the name of donation. The men and women I had met that day were bright, well-travelled, well-off people. If educated people like them behaved like this, what would uneducated people do?

But then I was reminded of an incident from my childhood. I was born and brought up in a village called Shiggaon in Karnataka's Haveri district. My grandfather was a retired schoolteacher and my grandmother, Krishtakka, never went to school. Both of them hardly travelled and had never stepped out of Karnataka. Yet, they were hard-working people, who did their work wholeheartedly without expecting anything from anybody in their life. Their photographs never appeared in any paper, nor did they go up on stage to receive a prize for the work they did. They lived like flowers with fragrance in the forest, enchanting everyone around them, but hardly noticed by the outside world.

In the village we had paddy fields and we used to store the paddy in granaries. There were two granaries. One was in the front and the other at the back of our house. The better-quality rice, which was white, was always stored in the front granary and the inferior quality, which was a little thick and red, was stored in the granary at the back.

In those days, there was no communal divide in the village. People from different communities lived together in peace. Many would come to our house to ask for alms. There were Muslim fakirs, Hindu dasaiahs who roamed the countryside singing devotional songs, Yellamma Jogathis who appeared holding the image of Goddess Yellamma over their heads, poor students and invalid people.

We never had too much cash in the house and the only help my grandfather could give these people was in the form of rice. People who receive help do not talk too much. They would receive the rice, smile and raise their right hand to bless us. Irrespective of their religion, the blessing was always 'May God bless you.' My grandfather always looked happy after giving them alms.

I was a little girl then and not too tall. Since the entrance to the front granary was low, it was difficult for grown-ups to enter. So I would be given a small bucket and sent inside. There I used to fill up the bucket with rice and give it to them. They would tell me how many measures they wanted.

In the evening, my grandmother used to cook for everybody. That time she would send me to the granary at the back of the house where the red rice was stored. I would again fill up the bucket with as much rice as she wanted and get it for her to cook our dinner.

This went on for many years. When I was a little older, I asked my grandparents a question that had been bothering me for long.

'Why should we eat the red rice always at night when it is not so good, and give those poor people the better-quality rice?'

My grandmother smiled and told me something I will never forget in my life.

'Child, whenever you want to give something to somebody, give the best in you, never the second best. That is what I have learnt from life. God is not there in the temple, mosque or church. He is with the people. If you serve them with whatever you have, you have served God.'

My grandfather answered my question in a different way.

'Our ancestors have taught us in the Vedas that one should:

'Donate with kind words.

'Donate with happiness.

'Donate with sincerity.

'Donate only to the needy.

'Donate without expectation because it is not a gift. It is a duty.

'Donate with your wife's consent.

'Donate to other people without making your dependants helpless.

'Donate without caring for caste, creed and religion.

'Donate so that the receiver prospers.'

This lesson from my grandparents, told to me when I was just a little girl, has stayed with me ever since. If at all I am helping anyone today, it is because of the teachings of those simple souls. I did not learn them in any school or college.

5

Lazy Portado

Portado was a young, bright, handsome and sweet boy from Goa. We were in B.V.B. College of Engineering at Hubli. He had been my classmate and lab partner throughout our course. So I knew him fairly well.

Portado had peculiar habits. Though he was intelligent, he was extremely lazy. Our theory classes were from eight in the morning till noon and lab was from two to five in the afternoon. Portado never came for the first class at eight. Occasionally, he turned up for the second or third hour but most of the time he only showed up for the last hour. He never missed our lab sessions, however.

In those days, attendance was not compulsory in college and our teachers were very lenient. They requested Portado to come on time but since there was no internal assessment, they couldn't really exercise their authority.

One day, I asked Portado, 'Why are you always late? What do you do at home?'

He laughed and said, 'I have a lot of things to do. I am so busy in the evenings that I can't get up before nine in the morning.'

47

'What things keep you so busy?" I asked him innocently.

'I meet my friends at night. We have long chats followed by dinner. You know, it takes a lot of time to build friendships. You will not understand. You people are all nerds. You only come to college to study.'

'Portado, you are a student. You should study, get knowledge, learn skills and work hard. Is that not important?'

'Oh, please. You remind me of my mother. Don't give me a sermon. Life is long. We have plenty of time. We should not learn anything in a hurry. We shouldn't be so stingy about time either.'

Then I noticed that he did not even have a watch since, for obvious reasons, he had no need for it.

Portado continued, 'In life, you need connections and networking. That can give you success. You can't network in a day. You have to spend time and money on building a network. Who knows? Some people that I meet now may make it big tomorrow and then that connection will work for me.'

I was a young girl from a middle-class and academic-minded family. I believed only in hard work. I never understood how networking could help.

During our college breaks, Portado would proudly tell us about his childhood: 'Oh, when I was young, I spent my time in big cities like Bombay, Delhi and Calcutta. In Calcutta, there are so many clubs. It is a matter of prestige to be a member of a club. When I start working, I want to be a member of all the good clubs in the city.' Every now and then, Portado felt that Hubli was a small and boring town. So he regularly went to Belgaum to meet his friends and 'network' with them.

During exams, Portado worked like a donkey. He glass-traced most of my original drawings so that he did not have to think about the solutions to engineering problems himself. His glass-trace drawings were definitely better than the originals because they were neater and there were no wrinkles or pencil marks. He always got more than me in drawings. He even kept the question papers of previous years and made his own question papers by process of elimination. Instead of reading textbooks, he read guides to pass the exams. With all this, he always managed to pass in second class.

Once, the examiner caught him because in a survey drawing he told the examiner that the mark on his drawing was actually a big tree in the middle of a road. It was a survey of a town near Dharwad. Unfortunately, the examiner happened to be from that town and he knew that there was no tree on that road. He questioned Portado, who said with a serious face, 'Sir, I have done the survey myself. I sat below the tree, had my lunch and then I continued.'

Calmly, the examiner said, 'I can't see this tree in any of your classmates' original drawings. This is only a mosquito between the glass and the drawing that you have tried to cover up.'

Portado just managed to pass the exams that year. But he was not perturbed. He said, 'I am not scared of the exams or the marks. Today's nerds will be tomorrow's mid-level managers. A person with good networking will be their boss.'

Because of his attitude and undisciplined habits, even the college hostel refused to keep him. So he rented a small house near college and lived there like a king.

Once, our class planned a picnic trip to Belgaum. Since Portado was familiar with the city, we decided to take his opinion and help. The picnic committee members, including myself, went to his house around eleven on a Sunday morning. We all assumed that Portado would be awake. But to our surprise, he was still in bed. When he opened the door, he said sleepily, 'Oh, why have you come so early on a Sunday?' He was quite annoyed to see us. 'Well, I am awake now, so please come in.'

We went in but there was absolutely no place to sit. His clothes were all over the room and newspapers were scattered on the floor. In the kitchen, dirty dishes were piled up in the sink and they were stinking. There were fish bones everywhere. There was also a cat and a dog inside the house. They were well fed with Portado's leftovers. The windows were not open either. The bed sheet looked like it had not been changed for a year. I did not have the courage to go see his bathroom.

Portado felt neither perturbed nor guilty. He said, 'Make some space for yourselves and sit down.' Some people moved Portado's undergarments and made some space but I could not do that because I was a girl, so I simply stood. Portado brought a stool for me from his kitchen. It was very sticky. I was even more hesitant to sit on it than on his clothes. I told him, 'It is better that I stand.' Portado offered us tea but none of us had the guts to drink any.

When I asked him about planning the details of the picnic, he said, 'We can start at twelve in the afternoon. My friend owns a lodge so I can take you there. The next day, we can go to Amboli Falls. Then we can also go to Goa.' Portado made a ten-day programme. But most of us could not afford a ten-day accommodation in a hotel, nor could we skip class for so many days. So the plan fizzled out. We thanked him and left. When I turned back and looked, Portado had closed the door and probably gone back to bed.

Soon the final year came around. We all passed the examinations and parted ways. Some of us felt sad because we had become a big family in the last four years together. We did not know our destinations and knew that we may not meet again. Of course, as Portado said goodbye he told us, 'If you are ever in Goa, please come to my house.' But I seriously doubted that I would ever run into him again.

Many decades passed. Once, I went to Dubai to give a lecture. After the lecture, people came up to talk to me but there was one person who waited until everybody had left. Then he walked over to where I was sitting and smiled. I recognized the smile but I did not remember where I had seen him. The man was bald, fat, had a big paunch and was dressed very ordinarily. I thought that he might be a mid-level manager in a construction company. I meet many people in my field and it is difficult to remember everybody.

I asked him, 'What can I do for you, sir? Are you waiting for me?'

With a cracked voice, he said, 'Yes, I have been waiting for you for a long time.'

'Oh, I'm sorry, I didn't know that you were waiting. Do you have any work with me?' I said.

'Yes, I just wanted to tell you that you were right and I was wrong.'

I was puzzled. What did he mean? I had never even met him before. I hardly came to Dubai since we did not even have an office there.

'I didn't get your name, sir. May I know your name, please?' I asked.

His laugh was bittersweet. He said, 'I am Portado, your classmate.'

I was very happy to see him and shook his hand. 'Oh, Portado, I am seeing you after thirty-five years! It has been so long that I didn't recognize you. Physically, both of us have changed so much. It is nice to meet you. Stay back. If you are here, come for dinner tonight. I want to catch up,' I said.

Sadly, Portado said, 'Sorry, I don't have much time. I am in the night shift. But I can have a cup of tea with you.'

We went to the hotel restaurant and I ordered a cup of tea for him and juice for myself. I wanted to talk more. I started the conversation with great enthusiasm and could not hold my questions back. 'Portado, where are you working now? How long have you been in Dubai? Are you married? How many children do you have? By the way, how are your networking friends? Do you ever come to India?'

Portado stopped me. 'I know your work involves computers but mine does not. You are too fast for me. Just like a computer. But I am in construction. So bear with me since I am slow. I have been in Dubai for the last five years. Before that, I was in India in several small places in different companies. Of course, I am married. I have two daughters.'

I interrupted him. 'You could have brought them today. I would have liked to meet them.'

'Sorry, I can't bring them because they are not here. I am in the lower level of management. So I cannot afford to bring my family here. My two daughters are studying in India and are doing engineering. I can't even afford their education in this place.'

I did not know what to say. I had never imagined Portado would end up like this.

Now it was his turn to talk. 'Do you remember, when I was in college, I used to make fun of all of you? I spent all my time in networking. After I finished engineering, I didn't get a good job. The reason was very obvious. I did not have the knowledge or the ability to work hard. I looked down upon the two qualities that are the stepping stones to success. I knew that I wanted to go up and reach the top spot in a company but no one can just fly there. I knew what position I should be in but I did not know the route. I thought that a change of job would help, but instead it reduced my value in the market. None of my networking friends helped me. They dropped me like a hot potato. They thought that I was clinging on to them like a parasite. Some of them were like me and also looking for jobs. I always thought that I would come up with someone's help. I never thought that I should take my own help. Now I am old. I am trying to learn new things and make up for lost time. But it is not easy. The market has become extremely competitive. Youngsters in college have more knowledge and quickness. They also have time on their side. I have told my daughters, you should study, get knowledge, learn skills and work hard.'

Portado continued, 'Do you remember who said this to me? It was you.'

He looked at his watch and said, 'My time is up. I must leave.'

I wished him all the best.

He walked a few steps, then came back and said, 'That day, I called you a nerd. Today, I call you smart.'

And he left.

6

A Life Unwritten

It was the year 1943. My father was a young medical doctor posted at a small dispensary in a village known as Chandagad, located on the border of the two states of Maharashtra and Karnataka. It rained continuously for eight months there and the only activity during the remaining four months was tree cutting. It was a lesser-known and thinly populated village surrounded by a thick and enormous forest. Since British officers came to hunt in the jungle, a small clinic was set up there for their convenience. None of the villagers went there because they preferred using the local medicines and plants. So there was nobody in the clinic except my father.

Within a week of his transfer there, my father started getting bored. He was uprooted from the lively city of Pune to this slow and silent village where there seemed to be no people at all! He had no contact with the outside world—his only companion was the calendar on the wall. Sometimes, he would go for a walk outside but when he heard the roar of the tigers in the jungle nearby, he would get scared and walk back to the clinic as fast as he could. It was no wonder then that he was too afraid to step out at night because of the snakes that were often seen slithering on the ground.

One winter morning, he heard heavy breathing outside his main door and bravely decided to peep through the window. He saw a tigress stretching and yawning in the veranda with her cubs by her side. Paralysed with fear, my father did not open the door the entire day. On another day, he opened the window only to find snakes hanging from the roof in front of his house—almost like ropes.

My father wondered if he was transferred to the village as a form of punishment for something he may have done. But there was nothing that he could do to change the situation.

One night, he finished an early dinner and began reading a book by the light of a kerosene lamp. It was raining heavily outside.

Suddenly, he heard a knock on the door. 'Who could it be?' he wondered.

When he opened it, he saw four men wrapped in woollen rugs with sticks in their hands. They said to him in Marathi, 'Doctor Sahib, take your bag and come with us immediately.'

My father barely understood their rustic Marathi. He protested. 'But the clinic is closed, and look at the time!'

The men were in no mood to listen—they pushed him and loudly demanded that he accompany them. Quietly, my father picked up his bag and followed them like a lamb to the bullock cart waiting for them. The pouring rain and the moonless night disoriented him and while he didn't know where they were taking him, he sensed that the drive might take some time.

Using all the courage he had left, he asked, 'Where are you taking me?'

There was no reply.

It was a few hours before they reached their destination and the bullock cart came to a complete halt. By the light of a kerosene lamp, somebody escorted them. My father noticed the paddy fields around him and in the middle of it all, he saw a house. The minute he set foot in the house, a female voice said, 'Come, come. The patient is here in this room.'

For the first time since he had come to the village, my father felt that he could finally put his medical expertise to good use. The patient was a young girl, approximately sixteen years old. An old lady was standing near the girl who was obviously in labour. My father turned pale. He went back to the other room and told her family, 'Look, I haven't been trained in delivering a baby and I am a male doctor. You must call someone else.'

But the family refused to listen. 'That's not an option. You must do what needs to be done and we will pay you handsomely,' they insisted. 'The baby may be delivered alive or dead but the girl must be saved.'

My father pleaded with them. 'Please, I am not interested in the money. Let me go now.'

The men came close, shoved him inside the patient's room and locked the door from outside. My father became afraid. He knew he had no choice. He had observed and assisted in a few deliveries under the guidance of his medical college professors, but nothing more. Nervously, he started recalling his limited past experience and theoretical knowledge as his medical instincts kicked in.

There was no table in the room. So he signalled the old lady, who appeared to be deaf and dumb, to help him set up a makeshift table with the sacks of paddy grains around them. Then my father extracted a rubber sheet from his bag and laid it out neatly on top of the sacks.

He asked the girl to lie down on it and instructed the old lady to boil water and sterilize his instruments. By then, the contraction had passed. The girl was sweating profusely and the doctor even more. She looked at him with big, innocent, teary eyes and slowly began, 'Don't save me. I don't want to make it through the night.'

'Who are you?'

'I am the daughter of a big zamindar here,' she said in a soft voice. The rain outside made it hard for him to hear her. 'Since there was no high school in our village, my parents let me study in a distant town. There, I fell in love with one of my classmates. At first, I didn't know that I was pregnant, but once I found out, I told the baby's father who immediately ran away. By the time my parents learnt of what had happened, it was too late to do anything. That's why they sent me here to this godforsaken place where nobody would find out.'

She stopped as a strong contraction hit her.

After a few minutes, she said, 'Doctor, I am sure that once the baby is born, my family will kill the child and beat me violently.' Then she grabbed my father's arms as more tears gathered in her eyes. 'Please don't try to save the baby or me. Just leave me alone here and let me die. That's all I want.'

At first, my father didn't know how to respond. Then he said to her as gently as he could, 'I am a doctor and I can't let a patient die when I know that I can do something to save him or her. You mustn't discourage me from doing my duty.'

The girl fell silent.

The labour was hard, scary and long and finally, my father managed to deliver the baby successfully with the assistance of the old lady. The young girl was exhausted and sweaty at the end of the ordeal. She closed her eyes in despair and didn't even ask to see the baby. Hesitantly, she asked, 'Is it a boy or a girl?'

'It's a girl,' replied my father, while trying to check the baby's vitals.

'Oh my God! It's a girl!' she cried. 'Her life will be just like mine—under the cruel pressure of the men in the family. And she doesn't even have a father!' She began sobbing loudly.

But my father was busy with the baby and barely heard her.

Suddenly, the girl realized that something was wrong, 'Doctor, why isn't the baby crying?' When she didn't get a reply, she continued, 'I will be happy if she doesn't survive. She will be spared from a cursed life.'

My father held the baby upside down, gently slapped her and, instantly, the baby's strong cries filled the room. When the men outside heard the baby cry, they opened the door and instructed him, 'Doctor, get ready to leave. We will drop you back.'

My father cleaned up his patient, gathered his instruments and packed his bag. The old lady began cleaning the room. He looked at the troubled young girl and said, 'Take the baby and run away from this place if you can find it in your heart to do so. Go to Pune and look for Pune Nursing School. Find a clerk there called Gokhale and tell him that RH has sent you. He will help you get admission in a nursing course. In time, you will become a nurse and lead an independent life, with the ability to take care of your own needs. Raise your daughter with pride. Don't you dare leave her behind or else she will end up suffering like you. That's my most sincere advice for you.'

'But, doctor, how will I go to Pune? I don't even know where it is!'

'Go to the nearest city of Belgaum and then from there, you can take a bus to Pune.'

My father said goodbye to her and came out of the room.

An old man handed him one hundred rupees. 'Doctor, this is your fee for helping the girl with the delivery. I warn you—don't say a word about what happened here today. If you do, I will learn of it and your head will no longer be attached to the rest of your body.'

My father nodded, suddenly overtaken by a sense of calm. 'I'm sorry,' he said. 'I think I forgot my scissors in the room. I will need it tomorrow at the clinic.'

He turned around and went back inside and saw the young girl gazing at the sleeping newborn with tears in her eyes. When the old lady's back was turned towards him, my father handed over the money to the girl. 'This is all I have with me right now,' he said. 'Use it and do what I have told you.'

'Doctor, what is your name?' she asked.

'My name is Dr R.H. Kulkarni, but almost everyone calls me RH. Be brave, child. Goodbye and good luck.'

My father left the room and the house. The return journey was equally rough and he finally reached home at dawn. He was dead tired and soon, sleep took over. The next morning, his mind wandered back to his first patient in the village and his first earning. He became aware of his shortcomings and wished he was better qualified in gynaecology. However, his current shortage of funds made him postpone the dream for another day.

A few months later, he got married and shared his dream of becoming a gynaecologist with his wife.

Time passed quickly. He was transferred to different places in Maharashtra and Karnataka and had four children along the way. By the time he turned forty-two, the couple had carefully saved enough money for further education and my father decided to pursue his desire. So he left his family in Hubli and joined Egmore Medical College in Chennai, and fulfilled his dream of becoming a gynaecologist surgeon. He was one of the rare male gynaecologists at the time.

He went back to Hubli and started working at the Karnataka Medical College as a professor. His sympathetic manner towards the underprivileged and his genuine concern for the women and girls he treated made him quite popular—both as a doctor and as a teacher. The same concern reflected in his liberal attitude towards his daughters and he allowed them to pursue their chosen fields of education, which was unheard of in those days.

My father was an atheist. 'God doesn't reside in a church, mosque or temple,' he would often say. 'I see him in all my patients. If a woman dies during childbirth, then it is the loss of one patient for a doctor but for that child, it is the lifelong loss of a mother. And tell me, who can replace a mother?'

Despite his retirement, my father's love for learning did not diminish and he remained active.

One day, he went for a medical conference to another city. There, he met a young woman in her thirties. She was presenting cases from her experience in the rural areas. My father found her work interesting and went to tell her so after the presentation. 'Doctor, your research is excellent. I am quite impressed by your work,' he said.

'Thank you,' she said.

Just then, someone called out to my father, 'RH, we are waiting for you to grab some lunch. Will you take long?'

The young woman asked, 'What is your name, doctor?'

'Dr R.H. Kulkarni, or RH.'

After a moment of silence, she asked, 'Were you in Chandagad in 1943?'

'Yes.'

'Doctor, I live in a village around forty kilometres away from here. May I request you to come home right now for a brief visit?'

My father was unprepared for such an invitation. Why was she calling him to her house?

'Maybe some other time, doctor,' he replied, hoping to end the matter.

But the woman was persistent. 'You must come. Please. Think of this as a request from someone who has been waiting for you for years now.'

My father was puzzled by her enigmatic answer and still refused, but she pleaded with him. There was something in her eyes—something so desperate—that in the end, he gave in and accompanied her to the village.

On the way to the village, both of them exchanged ideas and she spoke animatedly about her work and her findings. As the two of them approached her residence, my father realized that the house was also a nursing home. He walked in through the front door and saw a lady in her fifties standing in the living room.

The young woman next to him said, 'Ma, this is Dr RH. Is he the one you have been waiting for all these years?'

The woman came forward, bent down and touched her forehead to my father's feet. He felt his feet getting wet from her tears. It was strange. Who were these women? My father didn't know what to do. He quickly bent forward, placed his hands on the older woman's shoulders and pulled her up.

'Doctor, you may not remember me but I can never forget you. Mine must have been your first delivery.'

Still, my father couldn't recognize her.

'A long time ago, you lived in a village on the border of Maharashtra and Karnataka. One night, there was a heavy downpour and you helped me—a young, unmarried girl then—through childbirth. There was no delivery table in the room, so you converted stacks of paddy sacks into a makeshift table. Many hours later, I gave birth to a daughter.'

In a flash, the memories came flooding back and my father recollected that night. 'Of course I remember you!' he said. 'It was the middle of the night and I urged you to go to Pune with your newborn. I think I was as scared as you!'

'You gave me a hundred rupees, which is what my family paid you for the delivery. It was a big amount in those days and still, you handed it all over to me.'

'Yes, my monthly salary was seventy-five rupees then!' added my father with a smile.

'You told me your last name but I couldn't hear it because of the deafening sound of the rain. I took your advice, went to Pune, found your friend Gokhale and became a nurse. It was very, very hard, but I was able to raise my daughter on my own. After such a terrible experience, I wanted my daughter to become a gynaecologist. Luckily, she shared my dream too. Today, she is a doctor and is also married to one and they practise here. At one point, I spent months searching for you but with no luck. Then we heard that you had moved to Karnataka after the reorganization of the state departments in 1956. Meanwhile, Gokhale also passed away and I lost all hope of ever finding you. I prayed to God to give me a chance to meet you and thank you for showing me the right path at the right time.'

My father felt like he was in a Bollywood movie and was enchanted by the unexplained mystery of life. A few kind words and encouragement had changed a young girl's life.

She clasped her hands together. 'We are so grateful to you, doctor. My daughter wanted to call you for the inauguration of the nursing home here and we were very disappointed at not being able to reach you then. Time has passed and now the nursing home is doing very well.'

My father wiped his moist eyes and looked around to see the name of the nursing home. He looked to the right and found himself staring at it—R.H. Diagnostic.

7

The Line of Separation

During my trip to Pakistan, I was part of a large group. Each person in the group was keen to visit one place or the other in that country. Some wanted to see Takshila, others Lahore, Islamabad or Karachi. One day, we were having a discussion about this and everyone was voicing his or her opinion loudly. I noticed only Mrs Roopa Kapoor was sitting quietly. She was a seventy-five-year-old lady from Chennai and did not speak much unless spoken to. So I asked if there was any place she wanted to visit.

Without any hesitation, she said, 'I have to visit Pindi.'

'Where is Pindi? Is it some small town or village? I don't think we will have the time to make a detour like that from our packed itinerary.' Roopa smiled at my ignorance and said, 'I meant Rawalpindi. It is called Pindi for short by those who stay there.' I was intrigued. 'How do you know? Have you ever stayed there?'

'I was born and brought up there,' she replied, and then slowly she told me the story of her life.

She had stayed in Rawalpindi till the age of nineteen, when she got married and settled down in Chennai. Now Chennai was her home and she could speak Tamil and make excellent Tamil dishes, like puliyogare and rasam, as well as any natural-born Tamilian. But she had always yearned to come back and see her childhood home if she ever got the chance.

Soon we reached Islamabad and I was surprised to find it surrounded by mountains, as cool as a hill station. Roopa saw my surprise and said, 'Islamabad is a new city. Rawalpindi is a sister city, but it is older. Islamabad was built after the Partition with wide roads, shopping centres and rose gardens. Pindi is only twenty-odd kilometres away from Islamabad.' By now the soft-spoken, introverted Mrs Kapoor had become quite garrulous. There was a spark in her eyes and she spoke non-stop. Many of us wanted to see Islamabad first, but she insisted on going on to Rawalpindi.

She needed a companion for the trip and I volunteered to go with her. She was now quite excited, and told me, 'I want to see the house I left fifty-seven years ago.'

'That's a good idea,' I said. Then I remembered the lovely bouquet of flowers I had been presented on landing at Islamabad which I was still carrying. 'I will present this to whoever is staying in your house now.'

She was touched.

As the car left Islamabad airport behind, Mrs Kapoor started pointing out the sights to me like a tour guide. She showed me an old building on the left side of the road in a crowded area and said, 'That used to be an electrical goods manufacturing factory. Its owner, Kewal Ram Sahani, was my father's friend. My friends and I would come to this house for Lakshmi puja during Diwali.'

I told the driver to slow down a little so that she could cherish the journey. The car passed Sadar Bazar and looking at an old building with many shops, she said, 'Here my father's cousin Ratan Sethi owned a jewellery shop along with his partner Maqbool Khan. It was known as Khan and Sethi. My wedding jewellery was made here.'

She continued pointing out various buildings, each holding some fond memory for her. But many a time the buildings she was looking for had changed to new skyscrapers and she got disoriented. Suddenly the car stopped. A tyre was punctured, and the driver said it would take him a while to fix it. Roopa was restless. She did not want to wait even a minute more than required. So she said, 'You change the tyre. In the meantime I will go and visit some of the old places. We will join you at the next main road. To go to the main road, you take a left turn and the first right turn. You wait for us there.'

She behaved as if she knew every inch of that area and I followed her quietly. We walked into a small lane. She explained, 'I have been here many times with my friends Fatima and Noor. This used to be known as Tailor's Road. My neighbour Mehboob Khan's wife Mehrunnisa Chachi was an expert in designing new embroidery patterns. We used to come and give the designs. Come, we will take a shortcut . . . That is where my uncle lived.'

By now she was talking more to herself and making her way with ease through the narrow lanes. We went to the next road. There were old houses on the road and she went into the first huge bungalow. She said, 'This was my uncle Motiram Rai's house and the next house was that of Allah Baksh. They were great friends and loved each other. I still remember whenever Allah Baksh Chacha planted a tree in his house, my uncle would plant the same. This mango tree here was planted on a Basant Panchami day. There was so much of joy in both houses. My grandmother prepared kheer and sent me to Allah Baksh's house with a jug full of it. While I was carrying that jug, I bumped into a young man and the hot kheer fell on his feet. I was so scared and embarrassed.'

'Did you know him?'

'Not then but later. I married him!'

She then looked up at the tree and said, 'This has become so old now.'

We walked in through the gate. There was no one around and I was afraid we would be stopped by someone for trespassing. But Roopa was least bothered. It was as if she was in a world of her own. She walked to the backyard while I stood hesitating in the front. A couple walked in and were visibly surprised to see a stranger standing in their garden, that too in a sari. It was also just then that I noticed a board hanging in front of the door. It said 'Dr Salim and Dr Salma: Dentist'.

I started apologizing and explained the situation to them. Their faces lost the look of suspicion as soon as I finished my story. Roopa was still looking at all the trees and remembering her childhood. The couple welcomed us courteously. 'Please sit down. Do join us for a cup of tea.' They pulled up two chairs.

By now I was feeling very awkward, disturbing them in the morning. But Dr Salim said, 'Please sit. We are glad you came. Our grandparents too were from Surat in Gujarat. They emigrated to Pakistan and I was born and brought up here. My parents talk with great nostalgia about Surati farsan, Parsi dhansak and khakra.'

Just to make conversation I said, 'It must be difficult maintaining such a large bungalow now.'

Dr Salim replied, 'We moved to this house some years back. You see, this house happens to resemble the one my parents lived in in Surat, and they made me promise that I would not break it and make apartments as long as I stayed here. Allah has been kind to us and we don't need the money. Our neighbour Allah Baksh's children sold their property long back and now there is a commercial complex.'

By then Roopa had finished wandering in the garden and I formally introduced her to the couple. She asked if she could see the house from the inside. Dr Salim agreed happily. 'After we purchased this house ten years ago we made very few modifications. It is perhaps in the same state as you last saw it,' he said.

I walked in with Roopa. She looked into the main room and said, 'This was where my grandfather used to sit and control the house.' Then she pointed to a coloured glass door and said Allah Baksh's wife had painted it for them. 'That was the window through which she would send dry fruits to my aunt', 'That was where we used to fly kites.' Every brick, every wall held a memory for her. Finally I reminded her that it was time we left. We walked back to the garden and said our goodbyes to the couple. Dr Salim handed us a packet. 'There is no time for you to eat, but I cannot send two elders away without offering anything. Please take this and if God is willing we will meet again.'

We came out of the house and when we reached the main road the car was there, having followed Roopa's directions. Now she wanted to see her own house.

She told the driver, 'Take a right turn from the *chauraha*. I know the way. The first building on the right side is Al-Ameen School for girls and a little farther there is a Jesus and Mary convent. A little ahead on the left side, there is a government boys' school. Next to that is the Idgah maidan. Next to that is a lane with five huge bungalows. Each plot is an acre in size. The first one belonged to Kewal Ram. Second to Mia Mehboob Khan and the third one to Sardar Supreet Singh. Fourth one to Rai Sahib and the fifth was ours . . .'

She talked on and the driver followed her directions. She was mostly right. Yes, the red brick building on the right was the Al-Ameen School for girls. The Jesus and Mary convent was now a Loyola College and the government boys' school had become a degree college. But the Idgah maidan was not there. Instead there was a shopping complex. The five beautiful bungalows she described were also missing. Instead there was a mass of shops, hotels and video libraries piled next to each other. Roopa became upset.

'Madam, are you sure it is the same road?' the driver asked politely.

'Of course I am sure. I was born here. I spent nineteen years here. You were not even born then. How can I make a mistake?'

She told him to stop the car and got off to search. She was sure the house was still there behind the new buildings. She was possessed, as if searching for a lost child, or a precious jewel.

'My house was yellow in colour and there were two storeys. It had an entrance from the right side. From my house I could see the Idgah maidan. Two years back a friend of mine who also stayed here came to see the place and she told me the house was still very much here.'

She turned to me and continued, 'You know, once I had unknowingly walked on the wet cement floor near the entrance of the house and my footmark stayed there forever. My father wanted to keep it as a reminder of me after I got married and went away. I can recognize my house without any trouble.' But there was no house of that description in that area, with the footmark in the entrance. I knew by this time that the house was not there. But Roopa was reluctant to accept it.

We stood in front of the building where she said her house used to be. It was a hotel and a chowkidar was sitting at the entrance.

I asked him, 'How old is this hotel?'

He got up and replied, 'It is only a year old.'

'How long have you been working here?'

'Ever since the old building was demolished and the construction started.'

Roopa was quiet now.

'Was there a two-storeyed yellow building here with the entrance on the right and footprints along the portico?'

'Yes. There was a building like that but I don't remember the footprints.'

Now I knew that Roopa's house had been demolished to make way for this hotel. I looked at the chowkidar and told him, 'That was my friend's house.'

'Oh, please come inside. So what if your house is not there? The hotel stands on the same land. I am sure my owner will be happy to receive you. Have a cup of tea and a samosa.'

I looked at Roopa but she was not listening to our conversation.

She took a handful of soil from the little patch of garden in front of the hotel and said, 'This is my land. This is my soil. My ancestors made this their home. They were born and burnt here. The land, the trees, the air, the water, everything was ours. We knew the customs, the culture and the food. One day, some person drew a line and created two nations. And suddenly we became foreigners in our own land. We had to leave and adopt some other place whose language, food and culture were alien to us. A single line made me a stranger to my own land. People who have been uprooted feel a special pain which no one else can understand.'

I was quiet. I could only imagine her agony. I held her hand and suddenly realized that the bouquet of flowers I had meant to give to the owners of her old house was lying on the front seat of the car, withering slowly in the December sunshine.

8

India, the Holy Land

Maya was a simple young lady who lived in the Tibetan settlement on the outskirts of Mundugod, near Hubli in north Karnataka. She used to teach the Tibetan language to the children in the camp, so they would not forget their roots. She was smart and hard-working.

My father was a doctor working in Hubli and he occasionally visited that settlement. If any of the Tibetans wanted further treatment, they would visit my father at the Government Hospital in Hubli. Maya too started visiting my father when she was expecting her first child.

Over the months she became quite friendly with all of us. Whenever she came to the hospital she would pay us a visit too. My mother would invite her for a meal and we would spend some time chatting.

In the beginning, we would be in awe of her and stare at her almost-white skin, dove eyes, the little flat nose and her two long, thin plaits. Slowly we accepted her as a friend and she graduated to become my knitting teacher. Her visits were sessions of knitting, chatting and talking about her life in the camp and back in her country for which she still yearned. Maya would describe her homeland to us with great affection, nostalgia and, at times, with tears in her eyes.

'Tibetans are simple people. We are all Buddhists but our Buddhism is of a different kind. It is called Vajrayana. There's been a lot of influence from India, particularly Bengal, on our country and religious practices. Even our script resembles Bengali.'

Her words filled me with a sense of wonder about this exotic land called Tibet and I would pester her to tell me more about that country. One day we started talking about the Dalai Lama.

'What is the meaning of Dalai Lama?' I asked.

'It means "ocean of knowledge". Ours is a unique country where religious heads have ruled for 500 years. We believe in rebirth and that each Dalai Lama is an incarnation of the previous one. The present Dalai Lama is the fourteenth . . . You know, India is the holy land of Buddha. Historically, we have always respected India. There is a nice story about how Buddhism came to Tibet through India . . .'

I could not wait to hear about this!

'Long ago there was a king in Tibet who was kidnapped by his enemies. They demanded a ransom of gold, equal to the weight of the king. When the imprisoned king heard this, he somehow sent word to his son: "Don't waste any gold to get me back. Instead, spend that money to bring good learned Buddhist monks from India. With their help, open many schools and monasteries so that our people can live in peace and gain knowledge."'

Months passed and Maya delivered a baby. After that our meetings became less frequent. But she succeeded in awakening within me a curiosity about Tibet and a great respect for Buddhism.

Recently I got a chance to visit Tibet and memories of Maya filled my mind. I knew I would be seeing a Tibet filled with the Chinese but nevertheless I was keen to go. Among the places I wanted to see was a Buddha temple in Yarlung Valley that she had described to me.

When I finally reached the valley, it was past midday. There was a cold wind blowing though the sun was shining brightly. The Brahmaputra was flowing like a stream here, nothing like the raging torrent in Assam. Snow-capped mountains circled the valley and there was absolute silence all around.

The monastery at Yarlung is supposed to be a famous pilgrimage spot, but I could see only a handful of people in the entire place. After seeing everything inside I sat down on the steps and observed the serene beauty of the place.

I noticed an old woman accompanied by a young man walking into the monastery. The woman was very old, her face was wrinkled and she walked slowly and weakly. She was wearing the traditional Tibetan dress and her hair was plaited. The young man on the other hand was dressed in the usual modern manner, in tight jeans and a body-hugging T-shirt. The woman started circumambulating the monastery using her stick for support while the man sat down on the steps like me.

When she finished, I realized the old lady was staring at me. Then she said something to the young man in Tibetan.

She looked tired by the end of her ritual and sat down on the steps. She said something to her companion again but he took little notice of her. So she slowly picked up her stick and came towards me. She sat down near me, took my hands and, saying something, gently raised them to her eyes and kissed them. Before I could say anything, she got up and started to walk away. But I noticed she was smiling, as if she had achieved a long-held desire. I realized there was a wetness where her eyes had touched my hand.

Now the young boy reluctantly came up to me and apologized. 'Please forgive my grandmother,' he said. 'She is from a village in the interior part of Tibet. She has never ventured out of her village. This is the first time she has come to Yarlung. I beg your pardon for her behaviour.'

He was talking to me in English with an Indian accent.

'How come you speak English like us?' I asked in surprise.

'My name is KeTsang. I was in India for five years. I studied at Loyola College in Chennai. Now I run a restaurant in Lhasa. People here like Indian food and movies. I accompanied my grandmother for her pilgrimage. She was thanking you.'

'But for what? I have not done anything for her!'

'That is true, but your country has. It has sheltered our Dalai Lama for so many years. He is a living god to us, particularly to the older generation. We all respect the Dalai Lama, but due to political reasons, we cannot express it in public. You might have seen that there isn't a single photo of his in any public place in the whole of Lhasa. He is the fourteenth, but we have paintings, statues and pictures only up to the thirteenth.'

I still did not understand the old lady's gesture. The grandson explained, 'She said, "I am an old lady and don't know how long I will live. If I don't thank you before I die, I will never attain peace. Let anyone punish me for this, it does not matter. It is a gift that I met an Indian today and was able to thank you for sheltering our Dalai Lama. Yours is truly a compassionate land."'

Her words eerily echoed Maya's from many years back. I could only look down at the wet spot on my hand and smile.

9

Bonded by Bisleri

The 26 January horror of Kutch in Gujarat is well known. Without any warning, Mother Earth opened her mouth and engulfed the people and their belongings. Overnight, rich people were reduced to the streets. But the spirit of the Kutchi people is admirable. They faced this disaster bravely and are still fighting to restore normalcy.

The media has to be congratulated for its role in the relief efforts. Within hours of the tragedy, all newspapers and television channels had zoomed in to cover the disaster and broadcast it all over the world. Along with India, the rest of the world participated in helping these unfortunate people. After all the rush of the TV crews and media people, hordes of NGOs and government officials landed up in Kutch. People started picking up their life from where they had left it. Life started to return to normal at a slow pace.

I went to visit these areas after some time, when the dust of propaganda had settled down, in order to see actual life. After all, the emotions had drained off and reality had become the priority.

Several small villages deep inside Kutch, away from the main road connecting Ahmedabad and Bhuj, had been badly affected by the earthquake. I was visiting these remote places in the deep interior when one of the tyres of my jeep went flat. Getting it fixed would take some time. My driver went to get this done.

I was alone and bored. I saw a few tents nearby. They were temporary sheds covered with blue plastic sheets. They were temporary houses, schools and health centres for the people residing in that area. Later, I heard that there were tent hotels as well.

Life was busy and people were getting on with their chores. As it was monsoon season, men and women were busy in the fields. It was very strange. For many years there had not been much rain in Kutch, but that year it had rained abundantly. Farmers were having a bumper crop. I suppose nature has its own method of justice. On the one hand she takes away something and on the other she gives something in return. Small children were playing in the dust happily.

I peeped into one of the nearby tents. A young girl, about fourteen years old, was cleaning grains and preparing to cook a meal. When she saw me, she rose with a smile and said, 'Please come in and sit down.'

As I wanted to see how they lived, I entered the shed. She gave me a charpoy to sit on. Inside the tent it was clean and neat. There was a thin partition made of an old sari. I understood from her conversation that her family was not from Kutch.

The girl offered me a glass of water. Though it was the monsoon season, the sun was hot, but I was a little hesitant to drink the water. Many thoughts flashed across my mind. If the water was not sterile, then I was at risk of contracting diseases like dysentery and jaundice. If I refused to accept the water, however, I knew I would hurt the girl's feelings. So I took the glass but did not drink the water.

The girl had a younger sister who might have been around twelve years old. There was a little boy sleeping in a home-made cradle. Outside, there was a temporary open kitchen where sabzi was being cooked. The elder one was making dough from wheat flour.

'It seems from your language that you are not Gujaratis. Where are you from?' I asked.

Smiling, the younger sister answered, 'We're not from Gujarat, we're from Mumbai.'

'Have you come here to visit your relatives?'

'No, we don't have any relatives here. This is our house. We have come here with our parents.'

I was very surprised by this answer because, normally, people flee areas afflicted by calamities, whereas these people had moved in. 'What is your father doing here?'

Both girls were eager to give me information. The elder one replied, 'My father used to beg in Mumbai at Mahim Creek, near the church. My mother used to sell candles at the church entrance.'

'What made you come here?'

'One day, we saw the news on TV and came to know that there had been an earthquake here. It was shown every hour on TV in the corner shop. My father said "Let's go" and we came here.'

'Who paid for your train tickets?'

'Nobody. We came here without tickets. The whole train was full of people. There were many people like us who have come. The entire station was heavily crowded. There was no ticket collector.'

'How did you come from the train station?'

'We didn't know anyone. But there were plenty of buses running between the station and Bhuj. There were many foreign volunteers. The buses were jam-packed. We also got into one of the buses and landed on the main road.'

'How did you come to this particular area?'

'There were many jeeps going from the main roads to all interior villages. On the main road, there was a convoy of trucks full of different relief materials. They used to unload materials on either side of the road. People who did not have anything would pick them up from the roadside. We also picked up some.'

'What were the materials on the roadside?'

'There were food articles, apples, biscuit packets, clothes, blankets and many more items. My father told each one of us to pick up what we could and we collected a lot. We had never seen so much in our life in Mumbai. Everything was in plenty.'

Children are innocent and they always tell the truth until they become adults and lies creep into their lives. One lies to boast, to show what he is not. But children are so confident. They never pretend to be what they're not. Naturally, the

Mumbai beggar's daughters described the whole scenario as if it was a very memorable event.

The elder one said much more than that. 'There were people crying, some of them in pain. Some had lost their children or parents. It was very sad to see. But there were plenty of people to help also. There were doctors working overnight. There were swamijis working like common men, distributing medicines. There were army people digging to build houses. There was no difference between day and night, the rich and the poor.

'Our position was better. We did not lose anybody, nor did we lose any material, because we never had anything to begin with. People who have something have to fear losing it, but people who don't have anything to lose have no such fear. My mother and father helped people and someone said that inside the villages there was nobody to help. There were jeeps constantly travelling between the villages and the main road. So we got into one of the jeeps and landed in this village. Some organization was giving bamboo, camping materials like tents, and other roofing materials, free to all those people who had lost their houses. As we had no home, we also got all the materials. Sometimes we got double because my mother was in one queue and my father in another.'

'What all have you got?'

'Plenty of food. We have been eating to our hearts' content every day and we have also been giving some to people who were unable to stand in the queue. We know what it is to be hungry.'

'Why did you settle here then?'

'My father had asthma in Mumbai. He was unable to breathe and on many days we would go hungry. Someone said it was due to the pollution. It might be true, because after we came here, he has been normal, because there's no pollution here. Anyway, we had also built our own house, so we decided to settle down.'

'What job does your father do here? Does he continue to beg?'

'No. We are self-sufficient now. He is working as a coolie in a nearby field. He earns Rs 100 a day. Our mother also does the same thing, so the income is doubled. We're comfortable. The earthquake has come like a boon to us.'

She asked her sister to get some tea and biscuits. She inquired, 'Which biscuits do you want?'

'Do you have a variety?' I asked, surprised.

She pulled the curtain aside and I was amazed to see the varieties of biscuit packets, cartons of Bisleri mineral water, utensils, steel trunks and other things.

'From the day of the earthquake, most of us here have been drinking only Bisleri water. It seems some foreign country has sent a shipful of it. What I have given you is also mineral water.'

I took the glass of water and immediately gulped it down.

10

In India, the Worst of Both Worlds

Monday is the first working day of the week and an extremely busy day in our offices. All emails and papers have to be processed and meetings held. Long lists of appointments inevitably fill up our diaries. In between appointments, unexpected callers invariably turn up. Secretaries sweat it out on Monday mornings. But we have to get past Monday to reach Sunday again.

I recall one such Monday. I was engrossed in checking and replying to my email when my secretary told me that there were two visitors who had come to meet me without an appointment.

I asked her, 'What is special about these visitors that you are letting them in without an appointment?' I have great confidence in my staff and their ways of screening visitors.

She replied in a low tone, 'Madam, one is a very old man who looks very pale and the other is a middle-aged person. They say it is very urgent and have been waiting for quite some time.'

'Send them in,' I said.

They came in and sat opposite me. The old man seemed more than seventy years old. He was looking weak, tired and worried. He carried a worn-out bag. He was in a pitiable condition. With him was a middle-aged man who also looked somewhat worried.

I came to the point immediately. 'Tell me, what is the matter?'

The old man did not talk but just looked at the younger man.

The middle-aged man said, 'Madam, I saw this old man sitting near a bus stop. It seems he does not have anybody. He wants some shelter. Unfortunately, he does not have any money.'

This middle-aged man wanted to go on with all kinds of explanations. I often come across people who beat around the bush quite unnecessarily. They never tell you what they want directly. As I am used to such things, I often cut them short even at the risk of sounding curt.

'What do you want me to do?' I asked outright.

'I have read a lot about your work. I want you to help this gentleman.'

'Do you have anybody?' I asked the old man.

Tears welled up in his eyes. In a low voice he said, 'No, I do not have anybody.'

'What about your family?'

'No, I do not have anybody.'

'Where were you working before?'

I asked many questions and he gave reasonably satisfactory replies.

I felt bad for the old man. He had no money and nobody to give him a helping hand. It was a sad case. I thought of an old-age home with which we had regular contact. I called this home and told them that I was sending an old man there and that he should be kept there until we decided what we could do for him. The middle-aged man said, 'Do not worry. I will go with him and leave him there. From there, I will go to my office.'

Then they left my office. Soon, I got lost in my world of work, visitors, vouchers, budgets and so on.

Not that I forgot the old man's case. Once in a while I would call the old-age home and inquire about him. They would tell me that he was fine. I never had time to think more about him. I used to send money every month to the old-age home.

One day, I got a call from the caretaker of the home saying that the old man was very sick and that they had admitted him to a hospital. Could I come in the evening?

I went to see the old man at the hospital that evening.

He was really unwell. The doctors felt his condition was critical and that he did not have long to live. I thought there might be somebody he wished to see at a time like this. Maybe not his own children, but perhaps a nephew or a sister or brother, at least a friend? Was there anybody we could inform?

I asked him, 'Do you want to see anybody? We will call whomever you want. Do you have anybody's phone number?'

With a trembling hand, he wrote down a number and gave it to me. We called the number and informed the person at the other end that the old man was critical. After some time, a person came to see him. He looked anxious and worried and went straight to the old man.

I thought I had seen this man before. I tried to jog my memory but in vain. I just couldn't remember why the old man's visitor seemed so familiar. Perhaps he resembled someone I had met on my travels.

Meanwhile, the doctor came out and told me that the old man had breathed his last. I felt sad. I neither knew him nor had any contact with him. But somehow I felt very sad.

After a few minutes, the visitor came out. He had tears in his eyes. He sat down quietly on a bench. The whole place was quiet and depressing. The caretaker, this visitor and I sat in the visitors' hall, waiting for the formalities to be completed.

The visitor asked, 'Where is the bag he had?'

'What bag?'

'This man came to the old-age home carrying a bag,' he said.

My interest quickened. How did the visitor know that there was a bag?

I sent a peon back to the old-age home to fetch the bag. When it arrived, the visitor was eager to open it, but I did not permit him.

'You may not open the bag unless you identify yourself. What is your relationship with this old man? I want to know how you knew about this bag.'

He seemed very upset with my questions. Maybe he didn't like a woman questioning him. In India, men often get upset when women raise questions that are inconvenient for them. They prefer women who do not question what they do. Fortunately, this trend is disappearing slowly.

'It was I who accompanied him and left him at this home,' said the man.

'Who are you?' I was very curious.

'I am his son.'

You can imagine how shocked I was. Now I remembered—he was the middle-aged man who had come to our office that Monday morning claiming that he had found the old man sitting near a bus stop.

I was very upset. 'Why did you lie to me?'

Of course he had a story to tell. 'I have problems at home,' he said. 'My wife never liked my father. She asked me to choose between her and him. At that time we read about your foundation. We thought then that our problem could be solved without money.' He said he had no choice but to appease his wife because it was she who owned the house they lived in.

'What a way to solve your problem!' I protested. 'We help people who are orphans, but not orphans with children.'

When the bag was finally opened we found three sets of old clothes in it, some medicines and a passbook. When I opened the passbook, I was astounded. The old man had a bank balance of more than a lakh of rupees. The old man had put down a nominee for the account—his son, the same son who had got rid of him. Here was a son who was heartless enough to pass off his father as destitute in order to admit him in an old-age home. Now, the same son had come to claim his father's money.

Though his son had not wanted to look after him and had made him lie to me that he had nobody in this world, the old man nevertheless had wanted his money to go to his son. It never would have occurred to him to give that money to the old-age home that had sheltered him in his last days.

In Western countries, when old people die in old-age homes, they often will their property to the home or the hospital that cared for them. This is for the benefit of other senior citizens. They do not bequeath their money to their children, nor do the children expect their parents to do so. But in India, we have the worst of both worlds: children neglect aged parents, and parents routinely leave their property to their children.

'It is shameful the way you and your father cooked up this drama for the sake of a few thousand rupees!' I told the man. 'And you are setting a bad example. Next time when a genuinely destitute person seeks help, we will be unwilling to offer it. The memory of people like you will stay on.'

He hung his head in shame.

11

How I Taught
My Grandmother to Read

When I was a girl of about twelve, I used to stay in a village in north Karnataka with my grandparents. Those days, the transport system was not very good, so we used to get the morning paper only in the afternoon. The weekly magazine used to come one day late. All of us would wait eagerly for the bus, which used to come with the papers, weekly magazines and the post.

At that time, Triveni was a very popular writer in the Kannada language. She was a wonderful writer. Her style was easy to read and very convincing. Her stories usually dealt with complex psychological problems in the lives of ordinary people and were always very interesting. Unfortunately for Kannada literature, she died very young. Even now, after forty years, people continue to appreciate her novels.

One of her novels, called *Kashi Yatre*, was appearing as a serial in the Kannada weekly *Karmaveera* then. It is the story of an old lady and her ardent desire to go to Kashi or Varanasi. Most Hindus believe that going to Kashi and worshipping

Lord Vishweshwara is the ultimate *punya*. This old lady also believed in this, and her struggle to go there was described in that novel. In the story there was also a young orphan girl who falls in love but there was no money for the wedding. In the end, the old lady gives away all her savings to help the girl, without going to Kashi. She says, 'The happiness of this orphan girl is more important than worshipping Lord Vishweshwara at Kashi.'

My grandmother, Krishtakka, never went to school so she could not read. Every Wednesday, the magazine would come and I would read the next episode of this story to her. During that time she would forget all her work and listen with the greatest concentration. Later, she could repeat the entire text by heart. My grandmother too never went to Kashi, and she identified herself with the novel's protagonist. So more than anybody else she was the one most interested in knowing what happened next in the story and used to insist that I read the serial out to her.

After hearing what happened next in *Kashi Yatre*, she would join her friends at the temple courtyard, where we children would also gather to play hide-and-seek. She would discuss the latest episode with her friends. At that time, I never understood why there was so much debate about the story.

Once I went for a wedding with my cousins to the neighbouring village. In those days, a wedding was a great event. We children enjoyed ourselves thoroughly. We would eat and play endlessly, savouring the freedom because all the elders were busy. I went for a couple of days but ended up staying there for a week.

When I came back to my village, I saw my grandmother in tears. I was surprised, for I had never seen her cry even in the most difficult situations.

What had happened? I was worried.

'Avva, is everything all right? Are you OK?'

I used to call her 'Avva', which means 'mother' in the Kannada spoken in north Karnataka.

She nodded but did not reply. I did not understand and forgot about it. In the night, after dinner, we were sleeping on the open terrace of the house. It was a summer night and there was a full moon. Avva came and sat next to me. Her affectionate hands touched my forehead. I realized she wanted to speak. I asked her, 'What is the matter?'

'When I was a young girl I lost my mother. There was nobody to look after and guide me. My father was a busy man and got married again. In those days people did not consider education essential for girls, so I never went to school. I got married very young and had children. I became very busy. Later I had grandchildren and always felt so much happiness in cooking and feeding all of you. At times I used to regret not going to school, so I made sure that my children and grandchildren studied well . . .'

I could not understand why my sixty-two-year-old grandmother was telling me, a twelve-year-old, the story of her life in the middle of the night. But I knew I loved her immensely and there had to be some reason why she was talking to me. I looked at her face. It was unhappy and her eyes were filled with tears. She was a good-looking lady who was usually always smiling. Even today I cannot forget the worried expression on her face. I leant forward and held her hand.

'Avva, don't cry. What is the matter? Can I help you in any way?'

'Yes, I need your help. You know when you were away, *Karmaveera* came as usual. I opened the magazine. I saw the picture that accompanies the story of *Kashi Yatre* and I could not understand anything that was written. Many times I rubbed my hands over the pages wishing they could understand what was written. But I knew it was not possible.

'If only I was educated enough. I waited eagerly for you to return. I felt you would come early and read for me. I even thought of going to the village and asking you to read for me. I could have asked somebody in this village but I was too embarrassed to do so. I felt so dependent and helpless. We are well off, but what use is money when I cannot be independent?'

I did not know what to answer. Avva continued.

'I have decided I want to learn the Kannada alphabet from tomorrow. I will work very hard. I will keep Saraswati Puja day during Dasara as the deadline. That day I should be able to read a novel on my own. I want to be independent.'

I saw the determination on her face. Yet I laughed at her.

'Avva, at this age of sixty-two you want to learn the alphabet? All your hair is grey, your hands are wrinkled, you wear spectacles and you work so much in the kitchen . . .' Childishly I made fun of the old lady. But she just smiled.

'For a good cause if you are determined, you can overcome any obstacle. I will work harder than anybody, but I will do it. For learning there is no age bar.'

The next day onwards I started my tuition. Avva was a wonderful student. The amount of homework she did was amazing. She would read, repeat, write and recite. I was her only teacher and she was my first student. Little did I know then that one day I would become a teacher in computer science and teach hundreds of students.

The Dasara festival came as usual. Secretly I bought *Kashi Yatre* which had been published as a novel by that time. My grandmother called me to the puja place and made me sit down on a stool. She gave me the gift of a dress material. Then she did something unusual. She bent down and touched my feet. I was surprised and taken aback. Elders never touch the feet of youngsters. We have always touched the feet of God, elders and teachers. We consider that as a mark of respect. It is a great tradition but today the reverse had happened. It was not correct.

She said, 'I am touching the feet of a teacher, not my granddaughter; a teacher who taught me so well, with so much affection that I can read any novel confidently after such a short period. Now I am independent. It is my duty to respect a teacher. Is it not written in our scriptures that a teacher should be respected, irrespective of gender and age?'

I did return namaskara to her by touching her feet and gave my gift to my first student. She opened it and read immediately the title *Kashi Yatre* by Triveni and the publisher's name. I knew then that my student had passed with flying colours.

12

Rahman's Avva

Rahman was a young and soft-spoken employee who worked in a BPO. He was also an active volunteer in our Foundation. He would not talk without reason and would never boast about his achievements.

Rahman was a perfectionist. So any assignment given to him was done exceedingly well. He worked for the Foundation on the weekends and was very kind to the children in the orphanage. He spent his own money and always brought sweets for the children. I really liked him.

Since we worked closely together, he learnt that I am from north Karnataka, from Dharwad district. My language has that area's accent and my love for Dharwad food is very well known. One day, Rahman came and asked me, 'Madam, if you are free this Sunday, will you come to my house? My mother and sister are visiting me. Incidentally, my mother is also from Dharwad district. My family has read your columns in Kannada and your books too. When I told them that I am working with you, they expressed their earnest desire to meet you. Is it possible for you to have lunch with us?'

'Will you assure me that I'll get a good Dharwad meal?' I joked.

'I assure you, madam. My mother is a great cook.'

'Come on, Rahman. Every boy gives this compliment to his mother, however bad she may be at cooking. It is the mother's love that makes the food great.'

'No, she really is an amazing cook. Even my wife says so.'

'Then she must be really great because no daughter-in-law praises her mother-in-law's cooking without merit.' I smiled. 'By the way, which village in Dharwad district do they come from?'

He told me the name of a village near Ranebennur that I had never heard of. I happily agreed to visit them for lunch.

That Sunday, I took some flowers along. Rahman's newly constructed apartment was on Bannerghatta Road near the zoo. When I entered his home, I met his wife, Salma. She was a smart and good-looking girl. She worked as a teacher in the kindergarten nearby.

Then, he called out to his avva. A mother is usually referred to as 'avva' in north Karnataka. An old lady with grey hair came out of the kitchen. Rahman introduced her, 'This is my mother.' I was a bit surprised—she was not quite what I had expected. She was wearing a huge bindi the size of a 25-paisa coin and an Ilkal sari with lots of green bangles on both arms. She kept the sari *pallu* on her head. She had a contented smile on her face and with folded hands she said, 'Namaste.'

Rahman's sister entered from another room. She was so different from Rahman. Rahman was fair and very handsome.

His sister was tall and dark. She was wearing a cotton sari with a smaller bindi than her mother and also had two gold bangles on her hands. Rahman said, 'This is my sister Usha. She stays in Hirekerur. Both her husband and she are schoolteachers.'

I felt confused after meeting Rahman's mother and sister but I did not ask any questions.

After I sat down comfortably, Usha said, 'Madam, we love your stories because we feel connected to them. I teach some of your children's stories at school.'

Salma also joined the conversation. 'Even I like them, but my students are too young to understand.'

Rahman smiled and said, 'You must be surprised to see my mother and sister. I want to share my story with you.'

His mother went back to the kitchen and Usha started cleaning the table. Salma went to help her mother-in-law. Only the two of us remained.

'Madam, you must be wondering why my mother and sister are Hindus while I am a Muslim. Only you can understand and appreciate my life story because I have seen you helping people from all religions and communities without bias. I remember your comment to me: we can't choose the community or religion that we are born into, so we should never think that our community is our identity.'

Rahman paused, then continued, 'Madam, I believe in that too because I have also been brought up that way. I want to share my life and my perspective with you.'

Rahman started his story.

'Thirty years ago, Kashibai and Datturam lived on the outskirts of our village with their six-month-old daughter,

Usha. They looked after the ten-acre field of their landlord, Srikant Desai, who lived in Bombay. Srikant only came once a year to collect the revenue. The field was very large and it was too much for Kashibai and Datturam to handle. So, they requested the landlord to get another family to stay with them and help with the field. They also welcomed the thought of having company.

'Srikant contacted his acquaintances and found a suitable family. Soon, Fatima Bi and Husain Saab came to the village. They occupied one portion of the house and the other portion stayed with Kashibai and Datturam. Husain Saab and Datturam got along very well. However, Kashibai and Fatima Bi didn't see eye to eye at all. It is not that they were bad women but their natures were very different. Kashibai was loud, very frank and hard-working. Fatima Bi was quiet, lazy and an introvert. Inevitably; there was a fight. It all started with a hen. Kashibai's hen would come to Fatima Bi's portion of the house and lay eggs. Fatima Bi wouldn't return the eggs because she thought that her hen had laid them. Kashibai even tried colouring her hen to distinguish it from Fatima Bi's. Both the ladies shared a common well and would fight because both wanted to wash their vessels and clothes almost always at the same time. They also fought about their goats. Fatima Bi's goats came and ate Kashibai's flowers and leaves, which she used for her puja. Sometimes, Kashibai's goats went to Fatima Bi's place and left their droppings behind. Fatima Bi wouldn't return the droppings either.'

'What's so great about droppings?' I interrupted.

'Madam, goat droppings are used as manure.'

'Oh, I understand. Please continue,' I urged Rahman.

'The fights continued and sometimes Kashibai felt that she had made a mistake to tell their landlord that they wanted neighbours. She felt that she had been very happy without Fatima Bi. Fatima Bi also wanted to leave the farm and go to some other village but Husain Saab didn't agree. He would say, "You women fight about unnecessary things. This is a good opportunity for us to make money. The land is fertile and there is plenty of water. Our landlord is good and hardly visits. We can easily grow vegetables. Where can I get such work nearby? You should also become active like Kashibai and drop your ego. Try to adjust with her." The same conversation would happen on the other side of the house. Datturam would tell his wife, "Don't be so aggressive. You should mellow down like Fatima. Though she is lazy, she is good-natured."

'But as usual, both women never listened to their husbands.

'As time went by, Kashibai's daughter Usha turned two years old. Fatima Bi loved children and enjoyed watching Usha play in the field. Fatima Bi liked henna a lot. Every month, she coloured her hands with henna from the plant in the field and Usha always joined her. Usha was fascinated with the beautiful orange colour. She would come home and tell her mother, "Why can't you also colour your hands like Fatima Kaku?" (Kaku is equivalent to 'aunt' in the local language.)

'This comment irritated Kashibai. She said, "Fatima can afford to colour her hands because her husband works and also helps in the kitchen. She sits on the bed and listens to the radio. If I do that, will your father come and work in the kitchen?" Fatima Bi would overhear their conversation but still she continued her friendship with little Usha.

'When Fatima became pregnant, she became even lazier. She eventually reached full term and a distant relative came to help her with her delivery. A few days later, there was a festival in the village and Datturam and his family went to attend it. When they came back, Fatima Bi was not there. She was already in the hospital in critical condition and had delivered a son. The house was in complete silence. But the silence was deafening to Kashibai's ears. She started crying. She was very sad because Fatima Bi was in the hospital in such a serious condition. The next day, they learnt that Fatima Bi was no more.

'Husain Saab was left with his newborn son. The midwife stayed for a month and left. It was an uphill task for Husain Saab to look after a small baby. Neither Husain Saab nor Fatima Bi had any relatives who could take care of the little one. Most of them were coolies and a newborn child would only be a burden to the relatives. Datturam was very sympathetic and allowed Husain Saab to work less in the field but taking care of a small baby alone is very difficult.

'One night, the child started crying non-stop and Kashibai could not take it. She felt that enough was enough. After all, it was a little baby. A woman is so different from a man when it comes to rearing a child. Her motherly instinct made her go next door and tap on Husain Saab's door without even waiting for her husband. When Husain Saab opened the door, she told him, "Husain Saab, give me the baby. I am a mother. I know how to handle him." She picked up the baby boy, held him in her pallu and brought him to her house, holding him tightly to her chest. The baby boy stopped crying immediately. For the first time since the baby was born, Husain Saab slept through the night comfortably.

'The next day, Kashibai told Husain Saab, "I will look after this child until you get married again. Don't worry." She forgot her enmity with Fatima Bi and even felt ashamed. She thought that she should have been nicer to Fatima Bi. Now, Kashibai did not even bother about where the droppings of the goats fell or where the hens laid their eggs. For her, looking after the baby was more important. The baby was named Rahman and, to everyone's surprise, Husain Saab did not remarry. Rahman grew up in Kashibai's house and started calling her Avva and Usha became his akka. Rahman continued to sleep in his father's house but as soon as the sun rose, he ran to Kashibai's house to get ready. While Usha bathed on her own, Kashibai bathed little Rahman. She gave them breakfast, packed their lunches and walked them to school. Though Usha was two years older than Rahman, Kashibai made sure that they studied in the same class. Kashibai worked in the field in the afternoon and brought the children back in the evenings. Husain Saab cooked Rahman's dinner and Rahman would go back and sleep with his father at night. This continued for ten years.

'When Rahman was ten and Usha was twelve years old, Husain Saab fell ill and all his savings were spent on his treatment. Meanwhile, Kashibai purchased two she-buffaloes and started a milk business. She started earning more money than her husband.

'That same year, Husain Saab died of tuberculosis. Rahman was left all alone. There were hardly any people at Husain Saab's burial. A distant uncle came and told the mullah that he would take care of Rahman. But when the time came to take Rahman away, the uncle did not turn up at all. Without a second thought, Datturam and Kashibai took him in. Rahman was happy to stay in Kashibai's house.

'Kashibai was very conscious about Rahman's religion. Every Friday, she sent him for namaz and on holidays she sent him for Koran class at the local mosque. She told him to participate in all Muslim festivals even though there were very few Muslims in the village. Rahman also took part in the Hindu festivals celebrated in his house. Datturam and Kashibai bought two cycles for both the kids. Rahman and Usha cycled to high school and later they also rode their cycles to the same college.

'Eventually, they graduated and that day Kashibai told Rahman, "Unfortunately, we don't have a picture of your parents. So, turn towards Mecca and pray to Allah. Pray to Fatima Bi and Husain Saab. They will bless you. You are now grown up and independent. Usha is getting married next month. My responsibility to both Usha and you is now over."

'Kashibai's affection and devotion overwhelmed Rahman, who could not remember his own mother's face. He prayed to Allah and his parents and then touched Kashibai's feet. He said, "Avva, you are my ammi. You are my Mecca."

'Rahman got a job in a BPO in Bangalore and left home. He worked for different firms for a few years, saw growth in his career and started earning a good salary. He met Salma at a friend's wedding and fell in love with her.

'After getting Kashibai and Datturam's approval, he got married to Salma.'

When he finished his story, Rahman was very emotional and in tears.

I was amazed at Kashibai. She was uneducated but very advanced in human values. I was surprised and humbled by the largeness of her heart. Kashibai had raised the boy with his own religion and still loved him like her son.

By this time, lunch was ready and Usha invited me to eat. While having the delicious lunch, I asked Usha, 'What made you decide to visit here?'

'I have holidays at school and I took an extended vacation so I could come for Panchami.'

Panchami is a festival celebrated mostly by girls, particularly married women, who come to their brother's house. It is similar to the Rakhi festival in the north, where a brother acknowledges his sister's love. I recalled our history and remembered that Queen Karunavati had sent a rakhi to Emperor Humayun, seeking his protection.

Now, I looked at the wall in the dining room and for the first time I noticed two pictures in Rahman's house, one of Mecca and the other of Krishna, both hanging side by side.

13

Cattle Class

Last year, I was at the Heathrow Airport in London, about to board a flight. Usually, I wear a sari even when I am abroad, but I prefer wearing a salwar-kameez while travelling. So there I was—a senior citizen dressed in typical Indian apparel at the terminal gate.

Since the boarding hadn't started, I sat down and began to observe my surroundings. The flight was bound for Bengaluru and so I could hear people around me chatting in Kannada. I saw many old married couples of my age—they were most likely coming back from the US or UK after helping their children either through childbirth or a new home. I saw some British business executives talking to each other about India's progress. Some teenagers were busy with the gadgets in their hands while the younger children were crying or running about the gate.

After a few minutes, the boarding announcement was made and I joined the queue. The woman in front of me was a well-groomed lady in an Indo-Western silk outfit, a Gucci handbag and high heels. Every single strand of her hair was in place and a friend stood next to her in an expensive silk sari, pearl necklace, matching earrings and delicate diamond bangles.

I looked at the vending machine nearby and wondered if I should leave the queue to get some water.

Suddenly, the woman in front of me turned sideways and looked at me with what seemed like pity in her eyes. Extending her hand, she asked, 'May I see your boarding pass, please?'

I was about to hand over my pass to her, but since she didn't seem like an airline employee, I asked, 'Why?'

'Well, this line is meant for business-class travellers only,' she said confidently and pointed her finger towards the economy-class queue. 'You should go and stand there,' she said.

I was about to tell her that I had a business-class ticket but, on second thoughts, held back. I wanted to know why she had thought that I wasn't worthy of being in the business class. So I repeated, 'Why should I stand there?'

She sighed. 'Let me explain. There is a big difference in the price of an economy- and a business-class ticket. The latter costs almost two and a half times more than . . .'

'I think it is three times more,' her friend interrupted.

'Exactly,' said the woman. 'So there are certain privileges that are associated with a business-class ticket.'

'Really?' I decided to be mischievous and pretended not to know. 'What kind of privileges are you talking about?'

She seemed annoyed. 'We are allowed to bring two bags but you can only take one. We can board the flight from another, less-crowded queue. We are given better meals and seats. We can extend the seats and lie down flat on them. We always have television screens and there are four washrooms for a small number of passengers.'

Her friend added, 'A priority check-in facility is available for our bags, which means they will come first upon arrival and we get more frequent-flyer miles for the same flight.'

'Now that you know the difference, you can go to the economy line,' insisted the woman.

'But I don't want to go there.' I was firm.

The lady turned to her friend. 'It is hard to argue with these cattle-class people. Let the staff come and instruct her where to go. She isn't going to listen to us.'

I didn't get angry. The word 'cattle class' was like a blast from the past and reminded me of another incident.

One day, I had gone to an upscale dinner party in my home city of Bengaluru. Plenty of local celebrities and socialites were in attendance. I was speaking to some guests in Kannada, when a man came to me and said very slowly and clearly in English, 'May I introduce myself ? I am . . .'

It was obvious that he thought that I might have a problem understanding the language.

I smiled. 'You can speak to me in English.'

'Oh,' he said, slightly flabbergasted. 'I'm sorry. I thought you weren't comfortable with English because I heard you speaking in Kannada.'

'There's nothing shameful in knowing one's native language. It is, in fact, my right and my privilege. I only speak in English when somebody can't understand Kannada.'

The line in front of me at the airport began moving forward and I came out of my reverie. The two women ahead were whispering among themselves. 'Now she will be sent to the other line. It is so long now! We tried to tell her but she refused to listen to us.'

When it was my turn to show my boarding pass to the attendant, I saw them stop and wait a short distance away, waiting to see what would happen. The attendant took my boarding pass and said brightly, 'Welcome back! We met last week, didn't we?'

'Yes,' I replied.

She smiled and moved on to the next traveller.

I walked a few steps ahead of the women intending to let this go, but then I changed my mind and came back. 'Please tell me—what made you think that I couldn't afford a business-class ticket? Even if I didn't have one, was it really your prerogative to tell me where I should stand? Did I ask you for help?'

The women stared at me in silence.

'You refer to the term "cattle class". Class does not mean possession of a huge amount of money,' I continued, unable to stop myself from giving them a piece of my mind. 'There are plenty of wrong ways to earn money in this world. You may be rich enough to buy comfort and luxuries, but the same money doesn't define class or give you the ability to purchase it. Mother Teresa was a classy woman. So is Manjul Bhargava, a great mathematician of Indian origin. The concept that you automatically gain class by acquiring money is outdated.'

I left without waiting for a reply.

Approximately eight hours later, I reached my destination. It was a weekday and I rushed to office as soon as I could only to learn that my day was going to be spent in multiple meetings. A few hours later, I requested my program director to handle the last meeting of the day by herself as I was already starting to feel tired and jet-lagged.

'I am really sorry, but your presence is essential for that discussion,' she replied. 'Our meeting is with the organization's CEO and she is keen to meet you in person. She has been following up with me for a few months now and though I have communicated our decision, she feels that a discussion with you will change the outcome. I have already informed her that the decision will not be reversed irrespective of whom she meets, but she refuses to take me at my word. I urge you to meet her and close this chapter.'

I wasn't new to this situation and reluctantly agreed.

Time went by quickly and soon, I had to go in for the last meeting of the day. Just then, I received an emergency call.

'Go ahead with the meeting,' I said to the program director. 'I will join you later.'

When I entered the conference room after fifteen minutes, I saw the same women from the airport in the middle of a presentation. To my surprise, they were simply dressed—one was wearing a simple khadi sari while the other wore an unglamorous salwar-kameez. The clothes were a reminder of the stereotype that is still rampant today. Just like one is expected to wear the finest of silks for a wedding, social workers must present themselves in a plain and uninteresting manner. When they saw me, there was an awkward pause that lasted for only a few seconds before one of them acknowledged my presence and continued the presentation as if nothing had happened.

'My coffee estate is in this village. All the estate workers' children go to a government school nearby. Many are sharp and intelligent but the school has no facilities. The building doesn't even have a roof or clean drinking water. There are no benches, toilets or library. You can see children in the school . . .'

'But no teachers,' I completed the sentence.

She nodded and smiled. 'We request the foundation to be generous and provide the school with proper facilities, including an auditorium, so that the poor kids can enjoy the essentials of a big school.'

My program director opened her mouth to say something, but I signalled her to stop.

'How many children are there in the school?' I asked.

'Around 250.'

'How many of them are the children of the estate workers?'

'All of them. My father got the school sanctioned when he was the MLA,' she said proudly.

'Our foundation helps those who don't have any godfathers or godmothers. Think of the homeless man on the road or the daily-wage worker. Most of them have no one they can run to in times of crisis. We help the children of such people. The estate workers help your business prosper and in return, you can afford to help them. In fact, it is your duty to do so. Helping them also helps you in the long run, but it is the foundation's internal policy to work for the disadvantaged in projects where all the benefits go directly and solely to the underprivileged alone. Maybe this concept is beyond the understanding of the cattle class.'

Both the women looked at each other, unsure of how to respond.

I looked at my program director and said, 'Hey, I want to tell you a story.'

I could see from her face that she was feeling awkward. A story in the middle of a serious meeting?

I began, 'George Bernard Shaw was a great thinker of his times. One day, a dinner was arranged at a British club in his honour. The rules of the club mandated that the men wear a suit and a tie. It was probably the definition of class in those days.

'Bernard Shaw, being who he was, walked into the club in his usual casual attire. The doorman looked at him and said very politely, "Sorry, sir, I cannot allow you to enter the premises."

'"Why not?"

'"You aren't following the dress code of the club, sir."

'"Well, today's dinner is in my honour, so it is my words that matter, not what I wear," replied Bernard, perfectly reasonable in his explanation.

'"Sir, whatever it may be, I can't allow you inside in these clothes."

'Shaw tried to convince the doorman but he wouldn't budge from his stance. So he walked all the way back to his house, changed into appropriate clothes and entered the club.

'A short while later, the room was full, with people sitting in anticipation of his speech. He stood up to address the audience, but first removed his coat and tie and placed it on a chair. "I am not going to talk today," he announced.

'There were surprised murmurs in the audience. Those who knew him personally asked him about the reason for his out-of-character behaviour.

'Shaw narrated the incident that happened a while ago and said, "When I wore a coat and tie, I was allowed to come inside. My mind is in no way affected by the clothes I wear.

'"This means that to all of you who patronize the club, the clothes are more important than my brain. So let the coat and the tie take my place instead."

'Saying thus, he walked out of the room.'

I stood up. 'The meeting is over,' I said. We exchanged cursory goodbyes and I walked back to my room.

My program director followed me. 'Your decision regarding the school was right. But what was that other story all about? And why now? What is this cattle-class business? I didn't understand a thing!'

I smiled at her obvious confusion. 'Only the cattle-class folks will understand what happened back there. You don't worry about it.'

14

The Old Man and His God

A few years back, I was travelling in Thanjavur district of Tamil Nadu. It was getting dark, and due to a depression over the Bay of Bengal, it was raining heavily. The roads were overflowing with water and my driver stopped the car near a village. 'There is no way we can proceed further in this rain,' said the driver. 'Why don't you look for shelter somewhere nearby rather than sit in the car?'

Stranded in an unknown place among unknown people, I was a bit worried. Nevertheless, I retrieved my umbrella and marched out into the pelting rain. I started walking towards the tiny village, whose name I cannot recall now. There was no electricity and it was a trial walking in the darkness and the rain. In the distance I could just make out the shape of a small temple. I decided it would be an ideal place to take shelter, so I made my way to it. Halfway there, the rain started coming down even more fiercely and the strong wind blew my umbrella away, leaving me completely drenched. I reached the temple soaking wet. As soon as I entered, I heard an elderly person's voice calling out to me. Though

I cannot speak Tamil, I could make out the concern in the voice. In the course of my travels, I have come to realize that voices from the heart can be understood irrespective of the language they speak.

I peered into the darkness of the temple and saw an old man of about eighty. Standing next to him was an equally old lady in a traditional nine-yard cotton sari. She said something to him and then approached me with a worn but clean towel in her hand. As I wiped my face and head I noticed that the man was blind. It was obvious from their surroundings that they were very poor. The Shiva temple, where I now stood, was simple with the minimum of ostentation in its decorations. The Shivalinga was bare except for a bilwa leaf on top. The only light came from a single oil lamp. In that flickering light, a sense of calm overcame me and I felt myself closer to God than ever before.

In halting Tamil, I asked the man to perform the evening *mangalarati*, which he did with love and dedication. When he finished, I gave him a hundred-rupee note as the *dakshina*.

He touched the note and pulled away his hand, looking uncomfortable. Politely he said, 'Amma, I can make out that the note is not for ten rupees, the most we usually receive. Whoever you may be, in a temple, your devotion is important, not your money. Even our ancestors have said that a devotee should give as much as he or she can afford to. To me you are a devotee of Shiva, like everyone else who comes here. Please take back this money.'

I was taken aback. I did not know how to react. I looked at the man's wife expecting her to argue with him and urge him to take the money, but she just stood quietly. Often, in many households, a wife encourages the man's greediness. Here, it was the opposite. She was endorsing her husband's views. So I sat down with them, and with the wind and rain whipping up a frenzy outside, we talked about our lives. I asked them about themselves, their life in the village temple and whether they had anyone to look after them.

Finally I said, 'Both of you are old. You don't have any children to look after your everyday needs. In old age one requires more medicines than groceries. This village is far from any of the towns in the district. Can I suggest something to you?'

At that time, we had started an old-age pension scheme and I thought, looking at their worn-out but clean clothes, they would be the ideal candidates for it.

This time the wife spoke up, 'Please do tell, child.'

'I will send you some money. Keep it in a nationalized bank or post office. The interest on that can be used for your monthly needs. If there is a medical emergency you can use the capital.'

The old man smiled on hearing my words and his face lit up brighter than the lamp.

'You sound much younger than us. You are still foolish. Why do I need money in this great old age? Lord Shiva is also known as Vaidyanathan. He is the Mahavaidya, or great doctor. This village we live in has many kind people. I perform the puja and they give me rice in return. If either of us is unwell, the local doctor gives us medicines. Our wants are very few. Why would I accept money from an unknown person? If I keep this money in the bank, like you are telling me to, someone will come to know and may harass us. Why should I take on these worries? You are a kind person to offer help to two unknown old people. But we are content; let us live as we always have. We don't need anything more.'

Just then the electricity came back and a bright light lit up the temple. For the first time I saw the couple properly. I could clearly see the peace and happiness on their faces. They were the first people I met who refused help in spite of their obvious need. I did not agree with everything he had just said, but it was clear to me that his contentment had brought him peace. Such an attitude may not let you progress fast, but after a certain period in life it is required. Perhaps this world with its many stresses and strains has much to learn from an old couple in a forgettable corner of India.

15

A Lesson in Life from a Beggar

Meena is a good friend of mine. She is an LIC officer earning a good salary. But there was always something strange about her. She was forever unhappy. Whenever I met her, I would start to feel depressed. It was as though her gloom and cynicism had a way of spreading to others. She never had anything positive to say on any subject or about any person.

For instance, I might say to her, 'Meena, did you know Rakesh has come first in his school?'

Meena's immediate response would be to belittle the achievement. 'Naturally, his father is a schoolteacher,' she would say.

If I said, 'Meena, Shwetha is a very beautiful girl, isn't she?' Meena would be pessimistic. 'When a pony is young, he looks handsome. It is age that matters. Wait for some time. Shwetha will be uglier than anyone you know.'

'Meena, it's a beautiful day. Let's go for a walk.'

'No, the sun is too hot and I get tired if I walk too much. Besides, who says walking is good for health? There's no proof.'

That was Meena. She stayed alone in an apartment as her parents lived in Delhi. She was an only child and had the habit of complaining about anything and everything. Naturally, she wasn't very pleasant company and nobody wanted to visit her. Then one day, Meena was transferred to Bombay and soon we all forgot about her.

Many years later, I found myself caught in the rain at Bombay's Flora Fountain. It was pouring and I didn't have an umbrella. I was standing near Akbarallys, a popular department store, waiting for the rain to subside. Suddenly, I spotted Meena. My first reaction was to run, even in that pouring rain. I was anxious to avoid being seen by her, having to listen to her never-ending complaints. However, I couldn't escape. She had already seen me and caught hold of my hand warmly. What's more, she was very cheerful.

'Hey! I am really excited. It's nice to meet old friends. What are you doing here?'

I explained that I was in Bombay on official work.

'Then stay with me tonight,' she said. 'Let's chat. Do you know that old wine, old friends and memories are precious and rare?'

I couldn't believe it. Was this really Meena? I pinched myself hard to be sure it wasn't a dream. But Meena was really standing there, right in front of me, squeezing my hand, smiling, and yes, she did look happy. In the three years she had been in Bangalore, I had never once seen her smiling like that. A few strands of grey in her hair reminded me that years had passed. There were a few wrinkles on her face, but the truth was that she looked more attractive than ever before.

Finally, I managed to say, 'No, Meena, I can't stay with you tonight. I have to attend a dinner. Give me your card and I'll keep in touch with you. I promise.'

For a moment, Meena looked disappointed. 'Let's go and have tea at least,' she insisted.

'But Meena, it's pouring.'

'So what? We'll buy an umbrella and then go to the Grand Hotel,' she said.

'We won't get a taxi in this rain,' I grumbled.

'So what? We'll walk.'

I was very surprised. This wasn't the same Meena I had known. Today, she seemed ready to make any number of adjustments.

We reached the Grand Hotel drenched. By then the only thought in my mind was to find out who or what had brought about such a change in the pessimistic Meena I had known. I was quite curious.

'Tell me, Meena, is there a Prince Charming who has managed to change you so?'

Meena was surprised by my question. 'No, there isn't anyone like that,' she said.

'Then what's the secret of your energy?' I asked, like Tendulkar does in the ad.

She smiled. 'A beggar changed my life.'

I was absolutely dumbfounded and she could see it.

'Yes, a beggar,' she repeated, as if to reassure me. 'He was old and used to stay in front of my house with his five-year-old granddaughter. As you know, I was a chronic pessimist. I used to give my leftovers to this beggar every day. I never spoke to him. Nor did he speak to me. One monsoon day, I looked out of my bedroom window and started cursing the rain. I don't know why I did that because I wasn't even getting wet. That day I couldn't give the beggar and his granddaughter their daily quota of leftovers. They went hungry, I am sure.

'However, what I saw from my window surprised me. The beggar and the young girl were playing on the road because there was no traffic. They were laughing, clapping and screaming joyously, as if they were in paradise. Hunger and rain did not matter. They were totally drenched and totally happy. I envied their zest for life.

'That scene forced me to look at my own life. I realized I had so many comforts, none of which they had. But they had the most important of all assets, one which I lacked. They knew how to be happy with life as it was. I felt ashamed of myself. I even started to make a list of what I had and what I did not have. I found I had more to be grateful for than most people could imagine. That day, I decided to change my attitude towards life, using the beggar as my role model.'

After a long pause, I asked Meena how long it had taken her to change.

'Once this realization dawned,' she said, 'it took me almost two years to put the change into effect. Now nothing matters. I am always happy. I find happiness in every small thing, in every situation and in every person.'

'Did you give any gurudakshina to your guru?' I asked.

'No. Unfortunately, by the time I understood things, he was dead. But I sponsored his granddaughter to a boarding school as a mark of respect to him.'

16

May You Be the
Mother of a Hundred Children

I was on my way to the railway station. I had the nine o'clock Bangalore–Hubli Kittur Express to catch. Halfway to the station our car stopped. There was a huge traffic jam. There was no way we could either move forward or reverse the car. I sat and watched helplessly as a few two-wheelers scraped past the car through a narrow gap. Finally I asked my driver what the matter was. Traffic jams are not uncommon but this was something unusual. He got out of the car and said the road ahead was blocked by some people holding a communal harmony meet. I now realized it was perhaps impossible to get to the station. The papers had reported about the meeting and had warned that the roads would be blocked for some time. The car was moved into a bylane and seeing there was no way I could try and make my way back home, I decided to join the crowd and listen to the speeches.

From a distance, I could see the dais. There were various religious heads sitting on a row of chairs on the stage. An elderly gentleman stood next to me and commented loudly,

'All this is just a drama. In India, everything is decided on the basis of caste and community. Even our elections are dictated by them. Whoever comes to power thinks only of the betterment of his community. It is easy to give speeches but in practical life they forget everything.'

Just then a middle-aged lady started speaking into the mike. From the way she was speaking, so confidently, it was apparent that she was used to giving speeches and had the gift of the gab. Her analogies were quite convincing. 'When you eat a meal, do you eat only chapattis or rice? No, you also need a vegetable, a dal and some curd. The tastes of the dishes vary, but only when they are put together do you get a wholesome meal. Similarly different communities need to live together in harmony and build a strong country . . .' etc.

'It is a nice speech but who follows all this in real life?' the gentleman next to me commented.

'Why do you say that?' I had to ask finally.

He looked at me, surprised at my unexpected question, then answered, 'Because my family has suffered a lot. My son did not get a job as he was not from the right community, my daughter was transferred as her boss wanted to replace her with someone from his own community. It is everywhere. Wherever you go, the first thing people want to know is which caste or religion you belong to.'

The woman was still talking on the podium. 'What is her name?' I asked.

'She is Ambabhavani, a gifted speaker from Tamil Nadu.'

Her name rang a bell somewhere in my mind and suddenly I was transported away from the jostling crowds and the loud speeches. I was in a time long past, with my paternal grandmother, Amba Bai.

Amba Bai was affectionately called Ambakka or Ambakka Aai by everyone in the village. She spent her whole life in one little village, Savalagi, near Bijapur in north Karnataka. Like most other women of her generation she had never stepped into a school. She was married early and spent her life fulfilling the responsibilities of looking after a large family. She was widowed early and I always remember seeing her with a shaven head, wearing a red sari, the pallu covering her head always, as was the tradition in the then orthodox Brahmin society. She lived till she was eighty-nine and in her whole life she knew only the worlds of her ten children, forty grandchildren, her village and the fields.

Since we were farmers she owned large mud-houses with cows, horses and buffaloes. There was a large granary and big trees that cooled the house during the hot summers. There were rows of cacti planted just outside the house. They kept out the mosquitoes, we were told. Ajji (that's what we called Amba Bai) looked after the fields and the farmers with a passion. In fact, I don't recall her ever spending too much time in the kitchen making pickles or sweets like other grandmothers. She would be up early and after her bath spend some time doing her daily puja. She would make some jowar chapattis and a vegetable, and then head out to the fields. She would spend time there talking to the farmers about the seeds they had got, the state of the well or the health of their cattle. Her other passion in life was to help the women of the village deliver their babies.

Though I did not realize this till I was a teenager, Ajji was most unlike an orthodox Brahmin widow. She was very much for women's education, family planning and had much to say about the way society treated widows.

Those days there were few facilities available to the villages. There were a handful of medical colleges and not every taluk had a government hospital. In this scenario women who had borne children were the only help to others during childbirth. My grandmother was one of them. She was very proud of the fact that she had delivered ten perfectly healthy children, all of whom survived. And in turn, she would help others during their delivery, irrespective of caste or community. She always had a word of advice or a handy tip for the pregnant women of the village.

I would often hear such nuggets of wisdom from her.

'Savitri, be careful. Don't lift heavy articles. Eat well and drink more milk.'

'Peerambi, you have had two miscarriages. Be careful this time. Eat lots of vegetables and fruits. You should be careful but don't sit idle. Pregnancy is not a disease. You should be active. Do some light work. Send your husband Hussain to my house. I will give some sambar powder. My daughter-in-law prepares it very well.'

Of course, not everyone appreciated her advising them. One such person was Shakuntala Desai, who had stayed in the city for some time and had gone to school. 'What does Ambakka know about these things?' she would comment loudly. 'Has she ever gone to school or read a medical book? She is not a doctor.'

But Ajji would be least bothered by these comments. She would only laugh and say, 'Let that Shakuntala get pregnant. I will deliver the baby. My four decades of experience is better than any book!'

My father's job took us to various towns to live in, but we always came to Ajji's village during the holidays. They were joyous days and we would enjoy ourselves thoroughly.

Once, when we were at the village, there was a wedding in the neighbouring village. Ajji always refused to attend these social gatherings. That time, I too decided to stay back with her and one night there was only Ajji, me and our helper Dyamappa in that large house.

It was an unusually cold, moonless winter night in December. It was pitch dark outside. Ajji and I were sleeping together. Dyamappa had spread his bed on the front veranda and was fast asleep. For the first time that night, I saw Ajji remove her pallu from her head and the wisps of grey hair on her head. She touched them and said, 'Society has such cruel customs. Would you believe that I once had thick long plaits hanging down my back? How I loved my hair and what a source of envy it was for the other girls! But the day your grandfather died, no one even asked my permission before chopping off that beautiful hair. I cried as much for my hair as for my husband. No one understood my grief. Tell me, if a wife dies, does the widower keep his head shaved for the rest of his life? No, within no time he is ready to be a groom again and bring home another bride!'

At that age, I could not understand her pain, but now, when I recall her words, I realize how helpless she must have felt.

After some time she changed her topic. 'Our Peerambi is due any time. I think it will be tonight. It is a moonless night after all. Peerambi is good and pious, but she is so shy, I am sure she will not say anything to anyone till the pain becomes unbearable. I have been praying for her safe delivery to our family deity Kallolli Venkatesha and also at the Peer Saab Darga in Bijapur. Everyone wants sons, but I do hope there is a girl this time. Daughters care for parents wherever they are. Any woman can do a man's job but a man cannot do a woman's job. After your Ajja's death, am I not looking after the entire farming? Akkavva, always remember women have more patience and common sense. If only men realized that . . .'

Ajji had so many grandchildren she found it hard to remember all their names. So she would call all her granddaughters 'Akkavva' and grandsons 'Bala'.

As Ajji rambled on into the night, there was a knock on the door. Instinctively Ajji said, 'That must be Hussain.' And indeed it was. Ajji covered her head again and forgetting her griefs about widowhood, she asked quickly, 'Is Peerambi in labour?'

'Yes, she has had the pains since this evening.'

'And you are telling me now? You don't understand how precious time is when a woman is in labour. Let us go now. Don't waste any more time.'

She started giving instructions to Hussain and Dyamappa simultaneously.

'Hussain, cut the cactus, take a few sprigs of neem. Dyamappa, you light two big lanterns . . .

'Akkavva, you stay at home. Dyamappa will be with you. I have to hurry now.'

She was gathering some things from her room and putting them into her wooden carry-box. By that time, the huge Dyamappa, with his large white turban on his head and massive moustaches appeared at the door bearing two lanterns. In the pitch darkness he made a terrifying picture and immediately brought to my mind the Ravana in the Ramayana play I had seen recently. There was no way I was going to stay alone in the house with him! I insisted I wanted to go with Ajji.

Ajji was impatient. 'Akkavva, don't be adamant. After all, you are a teenage girl now. You should not see these things. I will leave you at your friend Girija's house.' But like any other teenager, I was adamant and would not budge from my decision.

Finally Ajji gave up. She went to the puja room, said a quick prayer and locked the house behind her. The four of us set off in pitch darkness to Hussain's house. Hussain lead the way with a lantern, Ajji, with me clutching on to her hand, followed, and Dyamappa brought up the rear, carrying the other lantern.

We made our way across the village. Ajji walked with ease while I stumbled beside her. It was cold and I did not know the way. All the time Ajji kept up a constant stream of instructions for Hussain and Dyamappa.

'Hussain, when we reach, fill the large drums with water. Dyamappa will help you. Boil some water. Burn some coal. Put all the chickens and lambs in the shed. See that they don't come wandering around . . .'

Finally we reached Hussain's house. Peerambi's cries of pain could be heard coming from inside.

Hussain and Peerambi lived alone. They were poor farm labourers who worked on daily wages. Their neighbour Mehboob Bi was there, attending to Peerambi.

Seeing Ajji, she looked relieved. 'Now there is nothing to worry. Ambakka Aai has come.'

Ajji washed her feet and hands and went inside the room with her paraphernalia, slamming the doors and windows shut behind her. Outside on the wooden bench, Hussain and Dyamappa sat awaiting further instructions from Ajji. I was curious to find out what would happen next.

Inside, I could hear Ajji speaking affectionately to Peerambi. 'Don't worry. Delivery is not an impossible thing. I have given birth to ten children. Just cooperate and I will help you. Pray to God to give you strength. Don't lose courage . . .' In between, she opened the window partly and told Hussain, 'I want some turmeric powder. I can't search in your house. Get it from Mehboob Bi's house. Dyamappa, give me one more big bowl of boiling water. Hussain, take a new cane tray, clean it with turmeric water and pass it inside. Dyamappa, I want some more burning coal . . .'

The pious, gentle Ajji was a dictator now!

The next few hours were punctuated by Peerambi's anguished cries and Ajji's patient, consoling words, while Hussain sat outside tense and Dyamappa nonchalantly smoked a bidi. The night got dark and then it started getting lighter and lighter. The cock, locked in its coop, crowed and with the rising sun we heard the sounds of a baby's crying.

Ajji opened one windowpane and announced, 'Hussain, you are blessed with a son. He looks just like your father, Mohammed Saab. Peerambi had a tough time but God is kind. Mother and child are both safe and healthy.'

S-l-a-a-m . . . the door shut again. But this time outside we grinned at each other in joy. Hussain knelt down and said a prayer of thanks. Then he jumped up and knocked on the door, wanting to see the baby. It remained shut. Ajji was not entertaining any visitors till she was done.

'Your clothes are dirty,' she shouted from inside. 'First have a bath, wear clean clothes and then come in, otherwise you will infect the baby and mother.'

Hussain rushed to the bathroom, which was just a thatched partition and poured buckets of clean water from the well on to himself.

Even after he rushed in, I could hear only Ajji's voice. 'Peerambi, my work is over. I have to rush home. Today is my husband's death ceremony. There are many rituals to be completed. The priests will arrive any time and I have to help them. I will leave now and if you want anything, send word through Hussain.

'Peerambi, to a woman, delivering a baby is like going to the deathbed and waking up again. Be careful. Mehboob Bi, please keep Peerambi's room clean. Don't put any new clothes on the baby. They will hurt him. Wrap him in an old clean dhoti. Don't kiss the baby on his lips. Don't show the baby to everybody. Don't keep touching him. Boil the drinking water and immerse an iron ladle in that. Peerambi should drink only that water. I will send a pot of home-made ghee and soft rice and rasam for Peerambi to eat . . . Now I have to go. Bheemappa is supposed to come and clean the garden today. If I am late, he will run away . . .'

By now she had allowed the window to be opened. I peeped in and saw the tired but joyous face of Peerambi and a tiny, chubby version of Mohammed Saab, Hussain's father, asleep on the cane tray. The neem leaves were hanging, the cactus was kept in a corner and the fragrance of the *lobana* had filled the entire room. Ajji also looked tired and there was sweat on her forehead. But she was cleaning her accessories vigorously in the hot water and wiping them before placing them carefully back in her wooden box.

Just as we were about to leave, Hussain bent down and touched Ajji's feet. In a choked voice he said, 'Ambakka Aai, I do not know how to thank you. We are poor and cannot give you anything. But I can thank you sincerely from the bottom of my heart. You are a mother of a hundred children. You have blessed my son by bringing him into this world. He will never stray from the correct path.'

Ajji touched him on his shoulder and pulled him up. There were tears in her eyes too. She wiped them and said, 'Hussain, God only wants us to help each other in difficult times. Peerambi is after all like another Akkavva to me.'

By now the sun was up and I followed Ajji back home without stumbling. Dyamappa was strolling lazily far behind us. One doubt was worrying me and I had to clear it. 'Ajji, you have given birth only to ten children. Why did Hussain say you are a mother of hundred?'

Ajji smiled and adjusting the pallu that was slipping off her head because of her brisk walk, she said, 'Yes. I have given birth only to ten children but these hands have brought out a hundred children in our village. Akkavva, I will pray that you become the mother of a hundred children, irrespective of the number you yourself give birth to.'

17

Food for Thought

Rekha is a very dear friend and our families have known each other for generations. Since I hadn't seen her for a long time, I decided to visit her. I picked up the phone and dialled her number.

Her father, Rao, who is like a father to me, picked up the phone. 'Hello?'

We exchanged greetings and I said, 'Uncle, I am coming to your house for lunch tomorrow.'

Her father, a botanist, was very happy. 'Please do. Tomorrow is a Sunday and we can relax a little bit. Don't run off quickly!' he replied.

In a city such as Bengaluru, going from Jayanagar to Malleswaram on a weekday usually takes a minimum of two hours. Travelling on a Sunday is much easier because it takes only half the time. When I reached her home the next day, I could smell that lunch was almost ready, and yet the aromas wafting in from the kitchen indicated to me that the day's menu would somehow be different. None of the typical

Karnataka dishes were laid out on the table, and the cuisine was, in fact, quite bland for my taste.

'I may wear a simple sari but I am a foodie, Rekha! Is the lunch specially arranged so that I don't come again?' I joked, as one can with an old friend who will not misunderstand and take offence.

Rekha's father laughed heartily. 'Well.' He sighed. 'Today is my mother's *shraddha* or death anniversary. On this day, we always prepare a meal from indigenous vegetables.'

'What do you mean by indigenous?' I was perplexed. 'Aren't all the vegetables available in our country indigenous, except perhaps ones like cauliflower, cabbage and potato?'

'Oh my God! You have just brought up the wrong topic on the wrong day with the wrong person!' exclaimed Rekha in mock dismay. 'After lunch, I think I should just leave you with my father and join you both later in the evening. This will take at least four hours of your time.'

I knew that Rekha's father was a botanist, but it was then that I realized that he was passionate about this subject. Though I had known him for a really long time, I had never seen this facet of his personality before. Probably, he had been too busy during his working years while we had been too busy playing and fooling around.

'Is this really true, Uncle?' I asked.

He nodded.

Since I come from a farmer's family on my paternal side, I have always had a fascination for vegetables. I knew vaguely about the things we could grow, the seasons to grow them in and the ones that we could not grow, including the reasons why. However, whenever I broached the subject with friends interested in agriculture and farming, I never really received a proper answer. Finally, here was a man more than willing to share his knowledge with me! I couldn't resist.

'You know, Rekha,' I said, 'it is difficult to get knowledgeable people to spend time explaining their subject matter to others. Today, Google is like my grandmother. I log on to the website any time I require an explanation of something I don't understand or want to learn about.'

'Right now, you are logging on to an encyclopedia,' Rekha smiled and glanced at her father affectionately.

The conversation drifted to other subjects as we ate lunch. The meal constituted of rice, sambar without chillies, dal with black pepper and not chillies, gorikayi (cluster beans), methi saag, cucumber raita and rice payasam. It was accompanied by udin vada with black pepper. There was pickle and some plain yogurt on the side too. After we had eaten this lunch, well-suited for someone recovering in a hospital, Rekha's father said, 'Come, let's go to the garden.'

Rekha's family owned an old house on the corner of a street. Her grandfather had been in the British railways and was lucky enough to buy the corner plot at a low price and had built a small home with a large garden there. In a city like Bengaluru, filled with apartments and small spaces, the garden was something of a privilege and a luxury.

Uncle and I walked to the garden while Rekha took a nap. He settled himself on a bench, while I looked around. It was a miniature forest with a large kitchen garden of carrots, okra, fenugreek and spinach—each segregated neatly into sections. A few sugar-cane stalks shone brightly in front of us while a dwarf papaya tree heavy with fruit stood in a corner. On the other end was a line of maize as well as flowering trees such as the parijata (the Indian coral tree), and roses of varying colours.

'Uncle and Aunty must be spending a lot of time here making this place beautiful,' I thought. 'All the trees and plants seem healthy—almost as if they are happy to be here!'

'Do you think that all the vegetables we have around us are from India? Or are they from other countries?' he asked out of the blue.

I felt as if I was back in school in front of my teacher. But I wasn't scared. Even if I gave him a wrong answer, it wasn't going to affect my progress report. 'Of course, Uncle! India has the largest population of vegetarians. So, in time, we have learnt to make different kinds of vegetarian dishes. Even people who eat meat avoid it during traditional events such as festivals, weddings, death anniversaries and the month of Shravana.'

'I agree with your assessment of everything, except that most vegetables are grown in India. The truth is that the majority of our vegetables are not ours at all. They have come from different countries.'

I stared at him in disbelief.

He pointed to a tomato plant—a creeper with multiple fruits, tied to a firm bamboo stick. 'Look at this! Is this an Indian vegetable?'

I thought of tomato soup, tomato rasam, tomato bhat (tomato-flavoured rice), sandwiches and chutney. 'Of course it is. We use it every single day. It is an integral part of Indian cuisine.'

Uncle smiled. 'Well, the tomato did not originate in India, but in Mexico. It made its way to Europe in 1554. Since nobody ate tomatoes over there at the time, they became ornamental plants because of the beautiful deep-red colour. At some point, there was a belief in Europe that it was good for curing infertility, while some thought that it was poisonous. The contradicting perspectives made it difficult for this fruit to be incorporated into the local diet for a long time. Its lack of value must have been a real push for initiating Spain's tomato festival, where millions of tomatoes are used every year to this day. A story goes that one business-savvy European surrounded his tomato plants with a sturdy, thick fence to show his neighbours that the fruits were not poisonous, but rather valuable and thus desirable. Gradually, the fruits reached India and began to be used as a commercial crop, thanks to its tempting colour and taste. It must have come to us during the reign of the British. But today, we cannot think of cooking without tomatoes.'

'Wow!' I thought. Out loud, I said, 'Uncle, tell me about an essential item that is used in our cooking but isn't ours.'

'Come on, try and guess. We simply cannot cook without this particular vegetable.'

I closed my eyes and thought of sambar, that essential south Indian dish, and the mutter-paneer typical of the north Indian cuisine. It took me a while to think of a common ingredient—the chilli. I brushed my thought away. 'No, there's no way that the chilli can be an imported vegetable. There can be no Indian food without it,' I thought.

Uncle looked at me. 'You are right. It is the chilli!' he exclaimed almost as if he had read my mind.

'How did you know?'

'Because people never fail to be shocked when they think of the possibility that chilli could be from another country. I can see it clearly on their faces when the wheels turn inside their head.'

My disbelief was obvious. How could we cook without chillies? It is as important as salt in Indian cooking.

'There are many stories and multiple theories about chillies,' Uncle said. 'When Vasco da Gama came to India, he came from Portugal via Brazil and brought many seeds with him. Later, Marco Polo and the British came to India. Thus, many more plant seeds arrived. The truth is that what we call "indigenous" isn't really ours. Think of chillies, capsicum, corn, groundnut, cashews, beans, potato, papaya, pineapple, custard apple, guava and sapodilla—they are all from South America. Over time, we indigenized them and learnt how to cook them. Some say that the chilli came from the country of the same name, while some others say it came from Mexico. According to a theory, black pepper was the ingredient traditionally used in India to make our food hot and spicy. Some scholars believe that the sole goal of the East India Company was to acquire a monopoly over India's pepper trade, which later ended in India's colonization. But when we began using chillies, we found that it tasted better than black pepper. To give you an example, we refer to black pepper as *kalu menasu* in Kannada. We gave a similar name to the chilli and called it *menasin kai*. In Hindi, it is frequently referred to as *mirchi*. In the war between black pepper and chilli, the former lost and chilli established itself as the new prince and continues to rule the Indian food industry even today. North Karnataka is famous for its red chillies now.'

'That much I do know, Uncle!' I closed my eyes and had a vision of my younger days. 'I remember seeing acres and acres of red-chilli plants during my childhood. The harvest used to take place during the Diwali season. I remember that Badgi district was dedicated to the sale of chillies. I had gone with my uncle one day and was amazed by the mountains of red-chillies I saw there.'

'Oh yes, you are right! Those red chillies are bright red in colour but they aren't really hot or spicy. On the contrary, chillies that grow in the state of Andhra Pradesh in the area of Guntur are extremely spicy. They are a little rounded in shape, not as deep red in colour and are called Guntur chillies. A good cook uses a combination of different kinds of chillies to make the dish delicious and attractive. Now that's what I call indigenous.'

'There were also two other kinds of chillies in our farm—one was a chilli called Gandhar or Ravana chilli that grows upside down and the other one, of course, was capsicum.'

Uncle nodded. 'Capsicum in India is nothing but green or red bell pepper in the West. But if you eat one tiny Ravana chilli, you will have to sit in the bathroom with your backside in pain and drink many bottles of water for a long, long time!

Or you will have to eat five hundred grams of candies, sweets or chocolates.'

We both laughed.

Hearing the laughter, Rekha's mother came and joined us. 'Are you folks joking about today's menu? I'm sorry that there wasn't much variety. When I heard that you were coming for lunch, I told Uncle to inform you that today's food was going to be bland and that you could come another Sunday, but he said that you are like family and wouldn't mind at all,' she said to me.

That sparked my interest. 'Tell me the reason for the bland food, Aunty!'

'We have a method to the madness, I guess. During death anniversaries, we do not use vegetables or spices that have come from other countries. Hence, we use ingredients like fenugreek, black pepper and cucumber, among others. Our ancestors were scared of using new vegetables and named these imports Vishwamitra *srishti*.'

This was the first time that I had heard of such a thing. 'What does that mean?'

Aunty settled into a makeshift chair under the guava tree. 'The story goes that there was a king called Trishanku who wanted to go to heaven along with his physical body. With his strong penance and powers, the sage Vishwamitra was able to send him to heaven, but the gods pushed him back because they were worried that it would set a precedent for people to come in with their physical bodies. That was not to be allowed. Vishwamitra tried to push Trishanku upwards but the gods pushed him down, like a game of tug of war. In the end, Vishwamitra created a new world for Trishanku and called it Trishanku Swarga. He even created vegetables that belonged neither to the earth nor heaven. So vegetables like eggplant and cauliflower are the creations of Vishwamitra, which must not be used at a time such as a dear one's death anniversary.'

Silence fell between us and I pondered over Aunty's story. After a few minutes, I saw Rekha coming towards us with some bananas and oranges and a box of what seemed to be dessert.

'Come,' she said to me, 'have something. The banana is from our garden and the dessert is made from home-grown ingredients too! You must be . . .'

Uncle interrupted, 'Do you know that we make so many desserts in India that aren't original to our country?'

'Appa, tell her the story of the guava and the banana. I really like that one,' Rekha said. She smiled as she handed me a banana.

Uncle grinned, pleased to impart some more knowledge. 'The seeds of guava came from Goa,' he said. 'So some people say that's how it was named. In Kannada, we call it *perala hannu* because we believe that it originated in Peru, South America. Let me tell you a story.

'Durvasa was a famed short-tempered sage in our ancient epics. He cursed anyone who dared to rouse his anger. The sage was married to a woman named Kandali. One day, she said to him, "O sage, people are terribly afraid of you while I have lived with you for such a long time. Don't you think I deserve a great boon from you?"

'Though Durvasa was upset at her words, he did not curse her. He thought seriously about what she had said and decided that she was right. "I will give you a boon. But only one. So think carefully," he said.

'After some thought, she replied, "Create a fruit for me that is unique and blessed with beautiful colours. The tree should grow not in heaven but on earth. It should have the ability to grow easily everywhere in our country. It must give fruits in bunches and for the whole year. The fruit must not have any seeds and must not create a mess when we eat it. When it is not ripe, we should be able to use it as a vegetable and once it is ripe, we should use it while performing pujas. We must be able to use all parts of the tree."

'Durvasa was surprised and impressed at the number of specifications his wife was giving him. He was used to giving curses in anger and then figuring out their solutions once he had calmed down, but this seemingly simple request was a test of his intelligence. "No wonder women are cleverer. Men like me get upset quickly and act before fully thinking of the consequences," he thought.

'The sage prayed to Goddess Saraswati to give him the knowledge with which he could satisfy his wife's demand. After a few minutes, he realized that he would be able to fulfil his wife's desire. Thus he created the banana tree, which is found all over India today. Every part of the tree—the leaf, the bark, the stem, the flowers and its fruits are used daily. Raw banana can be cooked while the ripe banana can be eaten easily by peeling off its skin. It is also an essential part of worship to the gods. The fruit is seedless and presents itself as a bunch. A mature tree lives for a year and smaller saplings are found around it.

'Kandali was ecstatic and named the plant *kandari*. She announced, "Whoever eats this fruit will not get upset, despite the fact that it was created by my short-tempered husband."

'Over a period of time, people started using the banana extensively and loved it. Slowly the name kandari changed to *kadali* and the banana came to be known as *kadali phala* in Sanskrit.' Uncle took a deep breath at the end of his story.

I smiled, amused at the story that seemed to result from fertile imagination. I had a strong urge to grab a banana and took one from the plate in front of me. 'You may have given me bland food today,' I said, 'but I really want some dessert.'

Rekha opened the box. It was filled with different varieties of sweets. I saw gulab jamuns, jhangri (a deep-fried flour-based dessert) and gulkand (a rose petal–based preserve). I can't resist gulab jamuns, so I immediately picked one up and popped it into my drooling mouth. It was soft and sweet. 'What a dessert!' I remarked, amazed at how delicious it was! 'Nobody can beat us Indians when it comes to desserts. I don't know how people can live in other countries without gulab jamuns.'

'Wait a minute, don't make such sweeping statements,' said Rekha. 'Gulab jamun is not from India.'

'Yeah, right,' I said, not convinced at all. Before she could stop me, I grabbed another gulab jamun and gulped it down.

'I'm serious. A language scholar once came to speak in our college. He told us that apart from English, we use multiple Persian, Arabic and Portuguese words that we aren't even aware of. Gulab jamun is a Persian word and is a dish prepared in Iran. It became popular in India during the Mughal reign because the court language was Persian. The same is true for jhangri, which is a kind of ornament worn on the wrist and the jhangri design resembles it.'

'You will now tell me that even gulkand is from somewhere else!' I complained loudly.

She grinned. 'You aren't wrong! Gulkand is a Persian word too—*gul* is nothing but rose and *kand* means sweet. Gul, in fact, originates from the word *gulab,* meaning rose.'

My brain was thoroughly exhausted with all this information. When I saw the oranges, I said with pride, 'I will not call this an orange now, but its Kannada name *narangi.*'

Uncle cleared his throat. 'Narangi is an Indian word but it does not originate in Karnataka. It is made up of two words—*naar*, which means orange or colour of the sun, and *rangi*, meaning colour.'

The conversation was making me feel truly lost.

'When people stay in one place for some time,' he continued, 'they unknowingly absorb the culture around them, including the regional food and language. At times, we adopt the changes into our local cuisine and make it our own. That's exactly what happened with the foods we have discussed.'

I glanced at my watch. It was time for me to leave. I thanked them profusely, especially Uncle, for enlightening me in a way that even Google could not.

There was a huge traffic jam despite it being a Sunday evening as I set out for home, but I wasn't bored on the way.

In fact, I was happy to recollect Uncle's words and perhaps, as a result, suddenly remembered an incident.

My mother had two sisters. Though all three sisters were married to men from the same state, their husbands' jobs were in different areas—one lived in south Karnataka in the old Mysore state, my parents lived in Maharashtra and the third stayed in the flatlands in a remote corner of Karnataka.

After their husbands retired, the three sisters lived in Hubli in the same area. It was fun to meet my cousins every day and eat meals together. We celebrated festivals as a family and the food was cooked in one house, though everybody brought home-cooked desserts from their own houses.

During one particular Diwali, we had a host of delicacies. My mother made puri and shrikhand (a popular dish in Maharashtra made from strained yogurt and sugar). My aunt from Mysore made kishmish kheer and a rice-based main course called bisi bele anna, while the other aunt made groundnut-based sweets such as jaggery-based sticky chikki and ball-shaped laddus.

As children, my cousins and I had plenty of fun eating them but in the car, I realized for the first time that all the sisters had absorbed something from the area that they had lived in. Despite their physical proximity, the food in each household was so diverse. I couldn't help but wonder how exciting the food really must be in the different regions of India.

I thought of paneer pizzas, cheese dosas and the Indian 'Chinese' food. They must have originated the same way. Who really said that India is a country? It is a continent—culturally vibrant, diverse in food and yet, distinctly Indian at heart.

18

Bombay to Bangalore

It was the beginning of summer. I was boarding the Udyan Express at Gulbarga railway station. My destination was Bangalore. As I boarded the train, I saw that the second-class compartment was jam-packed with people. Though the compartment was reserved, there were many unauthorized people in it. This side of Karnataka is popularly known as Hyderabad Karnataka since the Nizam of Hyderabad once ruled this area. There is scarcity of water here, which makes the land dry, and the farmers cannot grow anything during summer. Hence, many poor farmers and landless labourers from Hyderabad Karnataka immigrate to Bangalore and other big cities during the summer for jobs in construction. They return to their homes in the rainy season to cultivate their lands. This was April, so the train compartment was particularly crowded.

I sat down and was pushed to the corner of the berth. Though it was meant for three people, there were already six of us sitting on it. I looked around and saw students who were eager to come to Bangalore and explore different options to enhance their careers. There were merchants who were talking about what goods to order from Bangalore. Some government officers, though, were criticizing Gulbarga. 'What a place! Staying here is impossible because of the heat. No wonder people call this a punishment transfer!'

The ticket collector came in and started checking people's tickets and reservations. It was difficult to guess who had a ticket and who had a reservation. Some people had tickets but no reservation. This was an overnight train and people needed sleeper berths, but they were limited in number. People who did not have a reserved berth were begging the ticket collector to accommodate them 'somehow'. It was next to impossible for him to listen to everyone.

With his eagle eye, he easily located people who did not have a ticket. People without tickets were pleading, 'Sir, the previous train was cancelled. We had a reservation on that train. It is not our fault. We don't want to pay for this ticket again.' Another person was begging him: 'Sir, I was late to the station and there was a big queue. I didn't have time to buy a ticket. So, I got into this compartment.' The collector must have read the Bhagavad Gita thoroughly; he remained calm while listening to their stories and kept issuing new tickets for ticketless passengers.

Suddenly, he looked in my direction and asked, 'What about your ticket?'

'I have already shown my ticket to you,' I said.

'Not you, madam, the girl hiding below your berth. Hey, come out, where is your ticket?'

I realized that someone was sitting below my berth. When the collector yelled at her, the girl came out of hiding. She was thin, dark, scared and looked like she had been crying profusely. She must have been about thirteen or fourteen years old. She had uncombed hair and was dressed in a torn skirt and blouse. She was trembling and folded both her hands.

The collector asked again, 'Who are you? From which station did you get on? Where are you going? I can issue a full ticket for you with a fine.'

The girl did not reply. The collector was getting very angry since he had been dealing with countless ticketless passengers. He took out his anger on this little girl. 'I know all you runaways,' he shouted. 'You take a free ride in trains and cause tremendous problems. You neither reply to my questions nor pay for your ticket. I have to answer to my bosses . . .'

The girl still did not say anything. The people around the girl were not bothered at all and went about their business. Some were counting the money for their ticket and some were getting ready to get down at Wadi Junction, the next stop. People on the top berth were preparing to sleep and others were busy with their dinner. This was something unusual for me, because I had never seen such a situation in my vast experience of social work.

The girl stood quietly as if she had not heard anything. The collector caught hold of her arms and told her to get down at the next station. 'I will hand you over to the police myself. They will put you in an orphanage,' he said. 'It is not my headache. Get down at Wadi.'

The girl did not move. The collector started forcibly pulling her out from the compartment. Suddenly, I had a strange feeling. I stood up and called out to the collector. 'Sir, I will pay for her ticket,' I said. 'It is getting dark. I don't want a young girl on the platform at this time.'

The collector raised his eyebrows and looked at me. He smiled and said, 'Madam, it is very kind of you to offer to buy her a ticket. But I have seen many children like her. They get in at one station, then get off at the next and board another train. They beg or travel to their destination without a ticket. This is not an exceptional case. Why do you want to waste your money? She will not travel even with a ticket. She may leave if you just give her some money.'

I looked out of the compartment. The train was approaching Wadi Junction and the platform lights were bright. Vendors of tea, juice and food were running towards the train. It was dark. My heart did not accept the collector's advice—and I always listen to my heart. What the collector said might be true but what would I lose—just a few hundred rupees?

'Sir, that's fine. I will pay for her ticket anyway,' I said.

I asked the girl, 'Will you tell me where you want to go?'

The girl looked at me with disbelief. It was at this moment that I noticed her beautiful, dark eyes, which were grief-stricken. She did not say a word.

The collector smiled and said, 'I told you, madam. Experience is the best teacher.'

He turned to the girl and said, 'Get down.'

Then he looked at me and said, 'Madam, if you give her ten rupees, she will be much happier with that than with the ticket.'

I did not listen to him. I told the collector to give me a ticket to the last destination, Bangalore, so that the girl could get down wherever she wanted.

The collector looked at me again and said, 'But she won't get a berth and you will have to pay a penalty.'

I quietly opened my purse.

The collector continued, 'If you want to pay, then you should pay for the ticket from the train's starting point.'

The train originated from Bombay VT and terminated at Bangalore. I paid up quietly. The collector issued the ticket and left in disdain.

The girl was left standing in the same position. I asked my fellow passengers to move and give the girl some space to sit down because she now held a valid ticket. They moved very reluctantly. Then, I asked the girl to sit on the seat—but she did not. When I insisted, she sat down on the floor.

I did not know where to start the conversation. I ordered a meal for her and when the dinner box came, she held it in her hands but did not eat. I failed to persuade her to eat or talk. Finally, I gave the ticket to her and said, 'Look, I don't know what's on your mind since you refuse to talk to me. So, here's the ticket. You can get down wherever you want to.'

As the night progressed, people started sleeping on the floor and on their berths, but the girl continued to sit.

When I woke up at six o'clock the next morning, she was dozing. That meant that she had not got down anywhere.

Her dinner box was empty and I was happy that she had at least eaten something.

As the train approached Bangalore, the compartment started getting empty. Again, I told her to sit on the seat and this time she obliged. Slowly, she started talking. She told me that her name was Chitra. She lived in a village near Bidar. Her father was a coolie and she had lost her mother at birth. Her father had remarried and had two sons with her stepmother. But a few months ago, her father had died. Her stepmother started beating her often and did not give her food. I knew from her torn, bloodstained blouse and the marks on her body that she was telling the truth. She was tired of that life. She did not have anybody to support her so she left home in search of something better.

By this time, the train had reached Bangalore. I said goodbye to Chitra and got down from the train. My driver came and picked up my bags. I felt someone watching me. When I turned back, Chitra was standing there and looking at me with sad eyes. But there was nothing more that I could do.

As I started walking towards my car, I realized that Chitra was following me. I knew that she did not have anybody in the whole world. Now, I was at a loss. I did not know what to do with her. I had paid her ticket out of compassion but I had never thought that she was going to be my responsibility! But from Chitra's perspective, I had been kind to her and she wanted to cling on to me. When I got into the car, she stood outside watching me.

I was scared for a minute. 'What am I doing?' I questioned myself. I was worried about the safety of a girl in Wadi Junction station, but now I was leaving her in a big city like Bangalore—a situation worse than the previous one. Anything could happen to Chitra here. After all, she was a girl. There were many ways in which people could exploit her situation.

I told her to get into my car. My driver looked at the girl curiously. I told him to take us to my friend Ram's place. Ram ran separate shelter homes for boys and girls. We at the Infosys Foundation supported him financially on a regular basis. I thought Chitra could stay there for some time and we could talk about her future after I came back from my tours in a few weeks. There were about ten girls in the shelter and three of them were of Chitra's age. Most of the girls there already knew me.

As soon as I reached the shelter, the lady supervisor came out to talk to me. I explained the situation and handed Chitra over to her. I told Chitra, 'You can stay here for two weeks. Don't worry. These are very good people. I will come and see you after two weeks. Don't run away from here, at least until I come back. Talk to your lady supervisor. You can call her Akka.' (Akka means elder sister in the Kannada language.) I handed over some money to the supervisor and told her to buy some clothes and other necessary things for the girl.

After two weeks, I went back to the shelter. I was not sure if Chitra would even be there. But to my surprise, I saw Chitra looking much happier than before. She was having good food for the first time in her life. She was wearing new clothes and was teaching lessons to the younger children.

As soon as she saw me, she stood up eagerly. The supervisor said, 'Chitra is a nice girl. She helps in our kitchen, cleans the shelter and also teaches the younger children. She tells us that she was a good student in her village and wanted to join high school but her family didn't allow her to do so. Here, she is comfortable and wants to study further. What are your plans for her future? Can we keep her here?'

Soon, Ram also joined us. Ram knew the whole story and suggested that Chitra could go to a high school nearby. I immediately agreed and said that I would sponsor her expenses as long as she continued to study. I left the shelter knowing that Chitra had found a home and a new direction in her life.

I got busier with my work and my visits to the shelter reduced to once a year. But I always inquired about Chitra's well-being over the phone. I knew that she was studying well and that her progress was good.

Years went by. One day, Ram phoned me and said that Chitra had scored 85 per cent in her tenth class. When I went to the shelter to congratulate and talk to her, she was very happy. She was growing up to be a confident young woman. There was brightness in her beautiful, dark eyes.

I offered to sponsor her college studies if she wanted to continue studying. But she said, 'No, Akka. I have talked to my friends and made up my mind. I would like to do my diploma in computer science so that I can immediately get a job after three years.' I tried to persuade her to go to college for a bachelor's degree in engineering but she did not agree. She wanted to become economically independent as soon as possible. Somewhere inside me, I understood where she was coming from.

Three rainy seasons passed. Chitra obtained her diploma with flying colours. She also got a job in a software company as an assistant testing engineer. When she got her first salary, she came to my office with a sari and a box of sweets. I was touched by her gesture. Later, I got to know that she had spent her entire first salary buying something for everyone at the shelter.

Soon enough, Ram called me to discuss a new problem. 'Chitra is now a working girl. So she cannot stay in the shelter since it is only meant for students.' I told Ram that I would talk to Chitra and ask her to pay the shelter a reasonable amount of money per month towards rent. This way she could continue to stay there until she got married. I strongly felt that the shelter was a safe place for an unmarried, orphan girl like Chitra.

Ram asked me, 'Are you going to look for a boy for her?'

This was a new and an even bigger problem. As her informal guardian, I had to find a boy for Chitra or she herself had to find a life partner. This was a great responsibility. No wonder people say I have a penchant for getting into problems! But God also shows me unique ways of getting out of them. I told Ram, 'She is only twenty-one. Let her work for a few years. If you come across a suitable boy, please let me know.'

I called Chitra and gave her my opinion about her staying at the shelter, and she happily agreed to stay on and pay rent.

Days rolled by, and months turned into years. One day, when I was in Delhi, I got a call from Chitra. She was very happy. 'Akka, my company is sending me to the US! I wanted to meet you and take your blessings but you are not here in Bangalore.'

I was ecstatic for Chitra. I said, 'Chitra, you are now going to a different country. Take care of yourself and keep in touch. My blessings are always with you.'

Years passed. Occasionally, I received an email from Chitra. She was doing very well in her career. She was posted across several cities in the US and was enjoying life. I silently prayed that she should always be happy wherever she was.

Years later, I was invited to deliver a lecture in San Francisco for Kannada Koota, an organization where families who speak Kannada meet and organize events. The lecture was in a convention hall of a hotel and I decided to stay at the same hotel. After the lecture, I was planning to leave for the airport. When I checked out of the hotel room and went to the reception counter to pay the bill, the receptionist said, 'Madam, you don't need to pay us anything. The lady over there has already settled your bill. She must know you pretty well.'

I turned around and found Chitra there. She was standing with a young white man and wore a beautiful sari. She was looking very pretty with short hair. Her dark eyes were beaming with happiness and pride. As soon as she saw me, she gave me a brilliant smile, hugged me and touched my feet. I was overwhelmed with joy and did not know what to say.

'Chitra, how are you? I have not seen you for ages. What a sweet surprise. How did you know that I will be in this city today?'

'Akka, I live in this city and came to know that you are giving a lecture at the local Kannada Koota. I am also a member there. I wanted to surprise you. It is not difficult to find out about your schedule.'

'Chitra, I have so many questions to ask you. How is work? Have you visited India? And more importantly, have you found Mr Right? And why did you pay my hotel bill?'

'No, Akka. I haven't come to India since I left. If I come to India, how can I return without meeting you? Akka, I have something to tell you. I know that you were always worried about my marriage. You never asked me about my community. But you always wanted me to settle down. I know it is hard for you to choose a boy for me. Now, I have found my Mr Right. Please meet my colleague, John. We are getting married at the end of the year. You must come for our wedding and bless us.'

I was very happy to see the way things had turned out for Chitra. But I came back to my original question. 'Chitra, why did you pay my hotel bill? That is not right.'

With tears in her eyes and gratitude on her face, she said, 'Akka, if you hadn't helped me, I don't know where I would have been today—maybe a beggar, a prostitute, a runaway child, a servant in someone's house . . . or I may even have committed suicide. You changed my life. I am ever grateful to you.'

'No, Chitra. I am only one step in your ladder of success,' I said. 'There are many steps which led you to where you are today—the shelter which looked after you, the schools which gave you good education, the company which sent you to

America and, above all, it is you—a determined and inspired girl who made your life yourself. One step should never be given all the credit for the end result.'

'That is your thinking, Akka. I differ with you,' she said.

'Chitra, you are starting a new life and you should save money for your new family. Why did you pay my hotel bill?'

Chitra did not reply but told John to touch my feet. Then, suddenly sobbing, she hugged me and said, 'Because you paid for my ticket from Bombay to Bangalore!'

19

Miserable Success

Vishnu was a young, bright and ambitious student from the first batch I ever taught at college. So my relationship with him was closer than that with my students from subsequent batches. He was charming, communicative and clear in his thinking.

In college, we used to have long arguments on different issues and we used to agree to disagree on many matters. I used to tell him, 'Vishnu, I have seen many more seasons than you. With my experience in life, I want to tell you that having good relationships, compassion and peace of mind is much more important than achievements, awards, degrees or money.'

Vishnu would argue back: 'Madam, your stomach is full and you have achieved everything. Hence, you are comfortable in life and can say that. You have received many awards, so you don't care for them and you are not ambitious. You will never understand people like me.' Then, I usually just smiled at him. I liked him for his openness.

Vishnu was also very good at teaching. He completed his degree and got an excellent job in Microsoft in Seattle, USA. He was awaiting his visa to go abroad. I told him to teach at my college while he was waiting. Whenever I could not attend the laboratory sessions, I told him to take charge of the junior lab and be my substitute. He became very popular with the students.

I asked Vishnu, 'You are very good at teaching. Why don't you seriously think of becoming a professor?'

He said, 'My monthly salary in the US is more than a teacher's annual salary here. Why would I want to become a professor?'

'Vishnu, don't be so rude. A teacher is not respected for the salary but for his or her knowledge and teaching. If you don't respect the teaching profession, that is fine, but don't make such a comparison.'

Soon, Vishnu left the country on his new assignment.

Many years passed and a decade rolled by. My students, who were once young, were now middle-aged and I had gone from middle age to old age.

One day, my secretary told me that someone called Vishnu wanted to meet me. By this time, I knew many Vishnus and was not able to place him at once. She said that he was a student from my first batch of students. Now I recognized him instantly and told her to set up an appointment. After all, old wine, old memories and old students are precious in life.

On the day of the appointment, Vishnu walked in right on time. He had less hair than before and some of them were grey. He had put on weight. He was wearing an expensive shirt and there was a platinum diamond ring on his finger. But alas, his face was like a dried tomato. There was not a trace of enthusiasm on it. On the contrary, I could see some lines of worry on his face.

He sat in front of me and I ordered him a cup of tea. Vishnu looked at me and said, 'Madam, you look really old now.'

I smiled and said, 'Time and tide will wait for no one.' But he did not smile back. 'How are you, Vishnu?' I asked. 'I haven't met you for fifteen years. It is very nice of you to remember your old teacher and come to see me. Where are you? What are you doing now? Are you still with Microsoft?'

'No, madam. I left Microsoft after three years,' replied Vishnu.

'No wonder people say that if someone stays in a software company for more than three years, he is a loyal person!'

He did not respond to my joke. 'So where are you now?' I asked again.

'I own a company in Singapore. Two hundred people work for me. We make very good profit.' I felt Vishnu's voice had that pride of achievement, which was very natural.

'So you have settled in Singapore?'

'Not really, I come to India quite often because of work. I have a house in Vasant Vihar in Delhi, a flat in Worli in Mumbai, a bungalow in Raj Mahal Vilas Extension in Bangalore, a farm on Bannerghatta Road . . .'

I stopped him. 'Vishnu, I didn't ask you about your assets. I am not an income-tax person. I just wanted to know where you normally stay.' I was pulling his leg, yet he did not smile.

'Vishnu, you have told me enough about your financial assets,' I continued. 'Now tell me about your marital status. Are you married? How many children do you have? What do they do?' Usually, a mother and a teacher get the automatic authority to pose these questions to her children and students. I am no exception. Some people mind my questions because it is their personal life and I get the hint and stop. But most people happily tell me about their life.

'Yes, I am married. I have an eight-year-old daughter,' he said.

Vishnu pulled out his wallet and showed me his family photo. When he was in college, he used to go out with Bhagya, a girl junior to him. But the lady in the photograph was different. She was stunningly beautiful, like a model, and his daughter was cute.

I felt that his life was a picture-perfect postcard. He was successful, rich, had a very pretty wife and a daughter. What else can one want in life? With this kind of success, he should be very happy and enthusiastic—but he was not. I did not know the reason, but I knew that he would tell me. I stopped talking and allowed Vishnu to speak.

Slowly, Vishnu opened up. 'Madam, I have a problem. I have come to talk to you.'

'What problem? And why do you think I have the solution? Actually, a successful person like you should help an old teacher like me,' I joked to reduce the tension.

'It is nothing to do with success, madam. For the last few years, I have been feeling very sad. I feel like I am missing something in life. I can't pinpoint exactly what it is,' he said. 'Nothing makes me happy. Nothing even moves me or touches my heart, even if I see a heart-wrenching incident. I feel that I am travelling in a desert without water and the roads are paved with gold and silver . . .'

I asked him directly, 'Have you seen a doctor or a counsellor?'

'Of course I have. They said that a compassionate heart is important to enjoy life. They told me to read books and advised me to try and be happy by doing things such as looking at the sunrise, listening to the birds, taking long walks and exercising regularly.'

'Well, what happened?'

'I lost weight with all the activities but otherwise things didn't improve. I went back to a counsellor again. He told me to go to Somalia on a trip.'

'Why Somalia?' I was surprised. 'I know that there are trips to Europe, Hong Kong and Bangkok. But I have never heard of a trip to Somalia. Tell me, did you go there? What did you do in Somalia?' I was curious.

'Oh, they took us to orphanages, HIV camps and camps of children suffering from malnutrition. But nothing happened. I still didn't feel anything. On the contrary, my mind was busy calculating how Somalia could export to America or other European nations. What would you have done in my place, madam?' he questioned me.

'Don't put me in your shoes. What I would do is left to me and you don't have to do the same thing. Why can't you talk to someone who is very dear to you—maybe a friend or your wife or someone from your age group? They might be able to give you a better solution. After all, there is a generation gap between us.'

He was quiet. Then he said, 'Madam, all my life, I have calculated and made friendships. I have never spent time with people who aren't useful to me in some way. After all, life is a merciless, competitive field. Every move should take me one step higher on the ladder of success.'

I thought to myself, 'Now I know why Bhagya was replaced by the model wife.'

'How much time do you spend with your family?'

'My daughter is friendly but she is nice to me only when she wants something from me. Sometimes, I find it very strange. A child looks beautiful only with innocence but my daughter is more practical. My wife is very busy with the carpet business that she inherited from her father. She doesn't have any time to talk to me and my daughter, even though she works from home most of the time.'

He stopped for a second and continued, 'Or maybe I think that way. My wife wants to get all my contacts and clients so that she can expand her business. I am more of a database to her than a companion.'

I understood Vishnu's problem. Sometimes, it is very difficult to talk with your own family. I was touched that he felt safe coming to me. But he was expecting a quick fix from me. I was willing to listen to his problem, but that did not mean that I also had the solution.

Vishnu continued, 'Madam, tell me, how do I become compassionate? How do I build a strong family? How can I enjoy the sunrise and the moonlight? How much time does it take to get all these qualities? Are there any books or a crash course or people who can teach me? I don't care about the cost but it shouldn't take months together.'

I was shocked by his approach. 'Vishnu, compassion cannot be taught, sold or bought,' I said. 'There is no time limit either. It is one of the characteristics that you have to develop from the beginning. Understand that life is a journey. In that short journey, if you can show compassion to others, show it now. Our ancestors have always talked about the middle path for a reason. That path makes a person stable, happy and content. Vishnu, you are the role model for your children. Children will be what they see. What you have done, your daughter has copied.'

Vishnu sighed and said, 'Yes, madam. I understand what you are saying. I will take my daughter and work with poor people on a regular basis along with her. That will also help us bond. I am hoping that it will make me a better human being and I will be able to feel worthy again. Now I know what brought me to you. I cannot thank you enough.'

Vishnu left my office with hope in his heart and a smile on his face.

20

How to Beat the Boys

Recently, when I visited the US, I had to speak to a crowd of both students and highly successful people. I always prefer interacting with the audience, so I opened the floor to questions.

After several questions were asked, a middle-aged man stood up to speak. 'Madam, you are very confident and clear in communicating your thoughts. You are absolutely at ease while talking to us . . .'

I was direct. 'Please don't praise me. Ask me your question.'

'I think you must have studied abroad or done your MBA from a university in the West. Is that what gives you such confidence?' he asked.

Without wasting a second, I replied, 'It comes from my B.V.B.'

He seemed puzzled. 'What do you mean—my B.V.B.?'

I smiled. 'I'm talking about the Basappa Veerappa Bhoomaraddi College of Engineering and Technology in Hubli, a medium-sized town in the state of Karnataka in

India. I have never studied outside of India. The only reason I stand here before you is because of that college.'

In a lighter vein, I continued, 'I'm sure that the young people in the software industry who are present here today will appreciate the contribution of Infosys to India and to the US. Infosys has made Bengaluru, Karnataka and India proud. Had I not been in B.V.B., I would not have become an engineer. If I wasn't an engineer, then I wouldn't have been able to support my husband. And if my husband didn't have his family's backing, he may or may not have had the chance to establish Infosys at all! In that case, all of you wouldn't have gathered here today to hear me speak.'

Everyone clapped and laughed, but I really meant what I said. After the session got over and the crowd left, I felt tired and chose to sit alone on a couch nearby.

My mind went back to 1968. I was a seventeen-year-old girl with an abundance of courage, confidence and the dream to become an engineer. I came from an educated, though middle-class, conservative Brahmin family. My father was a professor of obstetrics and gynaecology at the Karnataka Medical College at Hubli, while my mother was a schoolteacher before she got married.

I finished my pre-university exams with excellent marks and told my family that I wanted to pursue engineering. I had always been fascinated with science, even more so with its application. Engineering was one of those branches of science that would allow me to utilize my creativity, especially in design. But it was as if I had dropped a bomb inside our house.

The immediate reaction was of shock. Engineering was clearly an all-male domain and hence considered a taboo for girls in those days. There was no questioning the status quo, wherein girls were expected to be in the company of other female students in a medical or science college. The idea of a woman entering the engineering field had possibly never popped up in anyone's mind. It was akin to expecting pigs to fly.

I was my grandmother's favourite granddaughter, but even she looked at me with disdain and said, 'If you go ahead and do this, no man from north Karnataka will marry you. Who wants to marry a woman engineer? I am so disappointed in you.' My grandmother never thought that I would do anything she disapproved of. However, she also didn't know that in the city of Mysore, across the river of Tungabhadra, lived a man named Narayana Murthy who would later want to marry me.

My grandfather, a history teacher and my first guru who taught me reading and writing, only mildly opposed it. 'My child, you are wonderful at history. Why can't you do something in this field? You could be a great scholar one day. Don't chase a dry subject like engineering.'

My mother, who was extremely proficient in mathematics, said, 'You are good at maths. Why don't you complete your post-graduation in mathematics and get a job as a professor? You can easily work in a college after you get married instead of being a hardcore engineer struggling to balance family and work.'

My father, a liberal man who believed in education for women, thought for a moment and said, 'I think that you should pursue medicine. You are excellent with people and languages. To tell you the truth, I don't know much about engineering. We don't have a single engineer in our family. It is a male-dominated industry and you may not find another girl in your class. What if you have to spend four years without a real friend to talk to? Think about it. However, the decision is yours and I will support you.'

Many of my aunts also thought that no one would marry me if I chose engineering. This would possibly entail my marrying somebody from another community, an absolutely unheard-of thing in those days.

However, I didn't care. As a student of history, I had read Hiuen Tsang's book *Si-Yu-Ki*. Before Tsang's travel to India, everybody discouraged him from making the journey on foot, but he refused to listen and decided to go. In time, he became famous for his seventeen-year-long journey to India. Taking courage from Tsang, I told my family, 'I want to do engineering. Come what may, I am ready for the consequences of my actions.'

I filled out the application form for B.V.B. College of Engineering and Technology, submitted it and soon received the news that I had been selected on the basis of my marks. I was ecstatic, but little did I know that the college staff was discomfited by this development.

The principal at the time was B.C. Khanapure, who happened to know my father. They both met at a barber shop one day and the principal expressed his genuine anguish at what he perceived to be an awkward situation. He told my father, 'Doctor Sahib, I know that your daughter is very intelligent and that she has been given admission only because of merit, but I'm afraid we have some problems. She will be the only girl in college. It is going to be difficult for her. First, we don't have a ladies' toilet on campus. We don't have a ladies' room for her to relax either. Second, our boys are young with raging hormones and I am sure that they will trouble her. They may not do anything in front of the staff but they will definitely do something later. They may not cooperate with her or help her because they are not used to talking to girls. As a father of four daughters, I am concerned about yours too. Can you tell her to change her mind for her own sake?'

My father replied, 'I agree with you, Professor Sahib. I know you mean well, but my daughter is hell-bent on pursuing engineering. Frankly, she's not doing anything wrong. So I have decided to let her pursue it.'

'In that case, Doctor Sahib, I have a small request. Please ask her to wear a sari to college as it is a man's world out there and the sari will be an appropriate dress for the environment she will be in. She should not talk to the boys unnecessarily because that will give rise to rumours and that's never good for a girl in our society. Also, tell her to avoid going to the college canteen and spending time there with the boys.'

My father came back and told me about this conversation. I readily agreed to all of the requests since I had no intention of changing my mind.

Eventually, I would become friendly with some of the boys, but I always knew where to draw the line. The truth is that it was these same boys who would teach me some of life's lessons later, such as the value of keeping a sense of perspective, the importance of taking it easy every now and then and being a good sport. Many of the boys, who are now older gentlemen, are like my brothers even after fifty years! Finally, it was the lack of ladies' toilets on campus that made me understand the difficulty faced by many women in India due to the insufficiency or sheer absence of toilets. Eventually, this would lead me to build more than 13,000 toilets in Karnataka alone!

Meanwhile, my mother chose an auspicious day for me to pay the tuition fee. It was a Thursday and happened to be the end of the month. My mother nagged me to pay the fee of Rs 400 that day although my father only had Rs 300 left. He told her, 'Wait for a few days. I will get my salary and then Sudha can pay her fees.'

My mother refused to budge. 'Our daughter is going to college. It is a big deal. We must pay the fees today—it will be good for her studies.'

While they were still going back and forth, my father's assistant, Dr S.S. Hiremath, came along with his father-in-law, Patil, who was the headman of Baad village near Shiggaon, the town where I was born. Patil curiously asked what was going on and my father explained the situation to him. He then took out his wallet and gave my father a hundred rupees. He said, 'Doctor Sahib, please accept this money. I want to gift it to this girl who is doing something path-breaking. I have seen parents take loans and sell their houses or farms to pay their sons' fees so that they can become engineers. In fact, sometimes, they don't even know whether their child will study properly or not. Look at your daughter. She desperately wants to do this and I think she is right.'

'No, Mr Patil,' my father refused. 'I can't take such an expensive gift. I will accept this as a loan and return it to you next month after I receive my salary.'

Patil continued as though he hadn't heard my father, 'The most important thing is for your daughter to do her best and complete her course and become a model for other girls.' Then he turned to me and said, 'Sudha, promise me that you will always be ethical, impartial and hard-working and that you will bring a good name to your family and society.'

I nodded meekly, suddenly humbled.

My first day of college arrived a month later. I wore a white sari for the first time, touched the feet of all the elders at home and prayed to Goddess Saraswati who had been very kind to me. I then made my way to the college.

As soon as I reached, the principal called me and gave me a key. He said, 'Here, Ms Kulkarni, take this. This is the key of a tiny room in the corner of the electrical engineering department on the second floor. You can use this room whenever you want.'

I thanked him profusely, took the key and immediately went to see the room. I opened the door excitedly, but alas! The room had two broken desks and there was no sign of a toilet. It was so dusty that I could not even consider entering it. Seeing me there, a cleaner came running with a broom in his hand. Without looking at me, he said, 'I'm so sorry. Principal Sahib told me yesterday that a girl student was going to join the college today, but I thought that he was joking. So I didn't clean the room. Anyway, I will do it right now.'

After he had finished cleaning, I still felt that the room was dusty. Calmly, I told him, 'Leave the broom here and give me a wet cloth, please. I will clean the room myself.'

After cleaning the room to my satisfaction, I brushed off the dust on my clothes and went to class.

When I entered the room on the ground floor, there were 149 pairs of eyes staring at me as though I were some kind of an exotic animal. It was true though. I was the 150th animal in this zoo! I knew that some of them wanted to whistle but I kept a straight face and looked around for a place to sit. The first bench was empty. As I was about to sit there, I saw that someone had spilt blue ink right in the middle of the seat. This was obviously meant for me. I felt tears threatening to spill over, but I blinked them away. Making use of the newspaper in my hand, I wiped the seat clean and sat on a corner of the bench.

I could hear the boys whispering behind me. One grumbled, 'Why the hell did you put ink on the seat? Now she may go and complain to the principal.'

Another boy replied, 'How can she prove that I have done it? There are 149 of us here.'

Despite feeling hurt, I did not go to the principal to complain. He had already warned my father that if I complained, these boys might persist in troubling me further and I may eventually have to leave the college. So, I decided to keep quiet no matter how much these boys tried to harass me.

The truth was that I was afraid of being so troubled by the boys' activities that I would quit engineering altogether. I thought of ways to stay strong—physically and mentally. It would be my *tapas*, or penance. In that instant, I resolved that for the next four years, I would neither miss any class nor ask anyone for help with class notes. In an effort to teach myself self-restraint and self-control, I decided that until I completed my engineering degree, I would wear only white saris, refrain from sweets, sleep on a mat and take baths with cold water. I aimed to become self-sufficient; I would be my best friend and my worst enemy. I didn't know then that such a quote already existed in the Bhagavad Gita where Krishna says, '*Atma aiva hi atmano bandhu aatma aiva ripu atmanah*'.

We really don't need such penance to do well in our studies, but I was young and determined and wanted to do all I could to survive engineering.

I had good teachers who were considerate and sought to look out for me in class. They would occasionally ask, 'Ms Kulkarni, is everything okay with you?'

Even our college principal, Professor Khanapure, went out of his way to inquire about my welfare and if any boys were troubling me.

However, I can't say the same about my classmates.

One day, they brought a small bunch of flowers and stuck it in my plaited hair without my knowledge when the teacher was not around. I heard someone shout from the back—'Ms Flowerpot!' I quietly ran my fingers through my hair, found the flowers and threw them away. I did not say anything.

At times, they would throw paper airplanes at my back. On unfolding the papers, I would find comments such as, 'A woman's place is in the kitchen or in medical science or as a professor, definitely not in an engineering college.'

Others would read, 'We really pity you. Why are you performing penance like Goddess Parvati? At least Parvati had a reason for it. She wanted to marry Shiva. Who is your Shiva?' I would keep the paper planes and refrain from replying.

There was a famous student-friendly activity in our college known as 'fishpond'. Rather than an actual fishpond, it was a fishbowl that carried a collection of anonymous notes, or the 'fish'. Anybody from the college could write a comment or an opinion that would be read out later on our college annual day. All the students would eagerly wait to hear what funny and witty remarks had been selected that year. The designated host would stand on the stage in the college quadrangle and read the notes out loud. Every year, most of the notes were about me. I was often the target of Kannada limericks, one of which I can still remember vividly:

Avva avva genasa,
Kari seeri udisa,
Gandana manege kalisa.

This literally translates to:

> Mom, Mom, there is a sweet potato,
> Please give me a black sari and send me to my husband's
>   house,
> This is because I'm always wearing a white sari.

Some of the romantic north Indian boys would modify the lyrics of songs from movies like *Teesri Kasam*:

> *Sajan re jhoot math bolo*
> *Sudha ke pass jaana hai*
> *Na haathi hai na ghoda hai*
> *Vahan paidal jaana hai.*

This can be translated as:

> Dear, come on, don't lie
> I want to go to Sudha
> I neither have an elephant nor a horse
> But I will go walking (to her).

All the boys would then sneak a glance at me to see my reaction, but I would simply hold back my tears and try my hardest to smile.

I knew that my classmates were acting out for a reason. It was not that they wanted to bully or harass me with deliberate intention as is the norm these days. It was just that they were unprepared—both mentally and physically—to deal with a person of the opposite sex studying with them. Our conservative society discouraged the mingling of boys and girls even as friends, and so, I was as interesting as an alien to them. My mind justified the reason for the boys' behaviour and helped me cope. And yet, the remarks, the pranks and the sarcasm continued to hurt.

My only outlet in college was my actual education. I enjoyed the engineering subjects and did very well in my exams. I found that I performed better than the boys, even in hardcore engineering subjects such as smithy, filing, carpentry and welding. The boys wore blue overalls and I wore a blue apron over my sari. I knew that I looked quite funny, but it was a small price to pay for the education I was getting.

When the exam results were announced, everyone else knew my marks before I did. Almost every semester, my classmates and seniors would make a singular effort to find out my marks and display them on the noticeboard for everyone to see. I had absolutely no privacy.

Over the course of my studies, I realized that the belief 'engineering is a man's domain' is a complete myth. Not only was I just as capable as them, I also scored higher than all my classmates. This gave me additional confidence and I continued to not miss a single day or a single class. I persisted in studying hard, determined to top the subsequent examinations. In time, I became unfazed that my marks were displayed on the noticeboard. On the contrary, I was proud that I was beating all the boys at their own game as I kept bagging the first rank in the university.

My ability to be self-sufficient made me strong and the boys eventually started to respect me, became dependent on me for surveys and drawings and asked me for the answers to the assignments. I began to make friends and even today, my good friends include Ramesh Jangal from the civil department, my lab partner Sunil Kulkarni, and Fakeer Gowda, M.M. Kulkarni, Hire Gowda, Anand Uthuri, Gajanan Thakur, Prakash Padaki, H.P. Sudarshan and Ramesh Lodaya.

I will never forget my teachers: L.J. Noronha from the electrical engineering department, Yoga Narasimha, a gifted teacher from Bangalore, Prof. Mallapur from the chemistry department, Prof. Kulkarni from hydraulics and many more. Between my classes, I also spent much time in the library and the librarian became very fond of me over time, eventually giving me extra books.

I also spoke frequently to the gardener about the trees that should be planted in front of the college, and during my four years there, I had him plant coconut trees. Whenever I go to B.V.B. now, I look at the coconut trees and fondly remember my golden days on the campus.

The four years passed quickly and the day came when I finally had to leave. I felt sad. I had come as a scared teenager and was leaving as a confident and bright young engineer! College had taught me the resilience to face any situation, the flexibility to adjust as needed, the importance of building good and healthy relationships with others, sharing notes with classmates and collaborating with others instead of staying by myself. Thus, when I speak of friends, I don't usually think of women but rather of men because I really grew up with them. When I later entered the corporate world, it was again dominated by men. It was only natural for my colleagues or friends to be men and only sometimes would there be women, whom I would get to know over many years.

College is not just a building made up of walls, benches and desks. It is much more intangible than that. The right education should make you a confident person and that is what B.V.B. did for me.

I later completed my master's programme from the Indian Institute of Science, Bangalore. Yet, B.V.B. continues to have a special place in my heart.

When my father passed away due to old age, I decided to do something in his memory. He had allowed me to go ahead and become an engineer, despite all odds and grievances he had heard from our family and society. Thus, I built a lecture hall in his memory in our college campus.

Whenever I go abroad to deliver a speech, at least five people of different ages come and tell me that they are from B.V.B. too. I connect with them immediately and can't help but smile and ask, 'Which year did you graduate? Who were your teachers? How many girls studied in your class?'

Now, whenever I go back to the college, it is like a celebration, like a daughter coming home. Towards the end of the visit, I almost always stand alone in the inner quadrangle of the stage. My memories take me back to the numerous occasions when I received awards for academic excellence. I then spend a few minutes in front of the noticeboard and walk up to the small room on the second floor of the electrical engineering department that was 'Kulkarni's Room', but no longer dusty. I remember the bench on which I sat and prepared for my exams. My heart feels a familiar ache when I recall some of my teachers and classmates who are no longer in this world today.

And then, as I walk down the stairs, I come across groups of girls—chatting away happily and wearing jeans, skirts or traditional salwar-kameez. There are almost as many girls as there are boys in the college. When they see me, they lovingly surround me for autographs. In the midst of the crowd and the signings, I think of my parents and my journey of fifty years and my eyes get misty.

May God bless our college, B.V.B.!

21

Three Thousand Stitches

We set up the Infosys Foundation in 1996. Unfortunately, I knew precious little about how things worked in a non-profit organization. I knew more about software, management, programming and tackling software bugs. Examinations, mark sheets and deadlines occupied most of my days. The concept behind the foundation was that it must make a difference to the common man—*bahujan hitaya, bahujan sukhaya*—it must provide compassionate aid regardless of caste, creed, language or religion.

As we pondered over the issues before us—malnutrition, education, rural development, self-sufficiency, access to medicine, cultural activities and the revival of the arts, among others—there was one issue that occupied my uppermost thoughts: the devadasi tradition that was pervasive throughout India.

The word devadasi means 'servant of the Lord'.

Traditionally, devadasis were musicians and dancers who practised their craft in temples to please the gods. They had a high status in society. We can see evidence of this in the caves of Badami, as well as in stories like that of the devadasi Vinapodi, who was very dear to the ruling king of the Chalukya dynasty between the sixth and seventh century in northern Karnataka. The king donated enormous sums of money to temples. However, as time went by, the temples were destroyed and the tradition of the devadasis fell into ruin. Young girls were initially dedicated to the worship and service of a deity or a temple in good faith, but eventually, the word 'devadasi' became synonymous with 'sex worker'. Some were born into the life, while others were 'sacrificed' to the temples by their parents due to various reasons, or simply because they caught a hair infection like the ringworm of the scalp, assumed to be indicative that the girl was destined to be a devadasi.

As I thought about their plight, I recalled my visit to the Yellamma Gudda (or Renuka temple) in Belgaum district of Karnataka years ago. I remembered their green saris and bangles, the smears of yellow *bhandara* (a coarse turmeric powder) and their thick, long hair as they entered the temple with goddess masks, coconuts, neem leaves and a *kalash* (a metal pot). 'Why can't I tackle this problem?' I wondered.

I didn't realize then that I was choosing one of the most difficult tasks for our very first project.

With innocence and bubbling enthusiasm, I chose a place in northern Karnataka where the practice was rampant and prostitution was carried on in the name of religion. My plan was to talk to the devadasis and write down their concerns to help me understand their predicament, followed by organizing a few discussions targeted towards solving their problems within a few months.

On my first day in the district, I armed myself with a notebook and pen and set out. I dressed simply, with no jewellery or bindi. I wore a pair of jeans, T-shirt and a cap. After some time, I found a group of devadasis sitting below a tree near a temple. They were chatting and removing lice from each other's hair.

Without thinking, I went up to them, interrupting their conversation. 'Namaskaram, Amma. I've come here to help you. Tell me your problems and I'll write them down.'

They must have been discussing something important because the women gave me a dirty look. They lobbed questions at me with increasing ferocity.

'Who are you? Did we invite you here?'

'Have you come to write about us? In that case, we don't want to talk to you.'

'Are you an officer? Or a minister? If we tell you our problems, how will you solve them?'

'Go away. Go back to where you came from.'

I did not move. In fact, I persisted. 'I want to help you. Please listen to me. Are you aware that there is a dangerous illness called AIDS that you could be exposed to? There is no cure for . . .'

'Just go,' one of them snapped. I glanced at their faces. They were furious.

But I did not leave. 'Maybe they need a little convincing,' I thought.

Without warning, one of them stood up, took off her chappal and threw it at me. 'Can't you understand simple Kannada? Just get lost.'

Insulted and humiliated, I felt my tears threatening to spill over. I turned back and fled.

Upon returning home, with the insult fresh on my mind, I told myself, 'I won't go there again.'

However, a few days later, it occurred to me that the women were probably upset about something else and that maybe I had simply chosen the wrong time and date to visit them.

So after another week, I went there again. This visit took place during the tomato harvest. The devadasi women were happily distributing small oval-shaped bright-red tomatoes to each other from the baskets kept near them. I approached them and smiled pleasantly. 'Hello, I've come to meet you again! Please hear me out. I really, really want to help you.'

They laughed at me. 'We don't need your help. But would you like to buy some tomatoes?'

'No, I am not very fond of tomatoes.'

'What kind of a woman are you? Who doesn't like tomatoes?'

I attempted to engage them once more. 'Have you heard of AIDS? You must know that the government is spending a lot of money on increasing awareness about it.'

'Are you a government agent? Or maybe you belong to a political party. How much commission are you getting to do this? Come on, tell us! We don't even have a proper hospital in this area and here you are, trying to educate us about a scary disease. We don't need your help. Our goddess will help us in difficult times.'

I stood dumbfounded, struggling to find words.

One of the women said decisively, 'This lady must be a journalist. That's why she has a pen and paper. She'll write about us and make money by exploiting us.' Upon hearing this, the others started throwing tomatoes at me.

This time, my emotions overpowered me and I started to cry. Sobbing, I fled from there once again.

I was in despair. 'Why should I work on this project? Why do they keep insulting me? Where else do the beneficiaries humiliate the person working for their well-being? I am not a good fit for this field. Yes, I should resign and go back to my academic career. The foundation can choose a different trustee.'

When I reached home, I sat down to compose a resignation letter.

My father came down the stairs and seeing me busy, with my head bent close to the paper, he asked, 'What are you writing so frantically?'

I narrated the entire episode to him.

To my amazement, rather than sympathizing with me, my father chuckled and said, 'I didn't know that you were so impractical.'

I stared at him in anger.

He took out an ice cream from the fridge and forced me to sit down and eat it. 'It'll cool your head,' he said and smiled.

After a few minutes, he said, 'Please remember. Prostitution has existed in society since ancient times and has become an integral part of life. It is one of the root problems of all civilizations. Many kings and saints have tried to eliminate it but no law or punishment has been successful in bringing it down to zero. Not one nation in the world is free of this. Then how can you change the entire system by yourself? You're just an ordinary woman! What you should do is reduce your expectations and lower your goal. For instance, try to help ten devadasis leave their profession. Rehabilitate them and show them what it means to lead a normal life. This will guarantee that their children will not follow in their footsteps. Make that your aim, and the day you accomplish it, I will feel very proud knowing that I gave birth to a daughter who helped ten helpless women make the most difficult transition from being sex workers to independent women.'

'But they threw chappals and tomatoes at me, Kaka,' I whined petulantly. I always called my father 'Kaka'.

'Actually, you got a promotion today—from chappals to tomatoes. If you pursue this and go there a third time, maybe you'll get something even better!' His joke brought a reluctant smile to my face.

'They won't even talk to me. Then how can I work for them?'

'Look at yourself,' my father said, dragging me in front of the nearest mirror. 'You are casually dressed in a T-shirt, a pair of jeans and a cap. This may be your style, but the common man and a rural Indian woman like the devadasi will never connect or identify with you. If you wear a sari, a *mangalsutra* [a married woman's holy necklace], put on a bindi and tie your hair, I'm sure that they will receive you much better than before. I'll also come with you. An old man like me will be of great help to you in such an adventure.'

I protested, 'I don't want to alter my appearance for their sake. I don't believe in such superficial changes.'

'Well, if you want to change them, then you have to change yourself first. Change your attitude. Of course, it's your decision in the end.'

He left me in front of the mirror and walked away.

My parents had never thrust their choices or beliefs on me or any of my siblings, whether it was about education, profession or marriage. They always gave their advice and helped us if we wanted, but we made all the choices.

For a few days, I was confused. I thought about the skills needed for social work. There was no glamour or money in this profession and I could not behave like an executive in a corporate house. I required language skills, of which English may not be needed at all! I had to be able to sit down on the floor and eat the local food, no matter where I travelled to for work. I had to listen patiently, and most of all, I should love the work I did. What would give me higher satisfaction— keeping my external appearance the way it was or the work that I would do?

After some introspection, I decided to change my appearance and concentrate completely on the work.

Before my next visit, I pulled my hair back, tied it and adorned it with flowers. I wore a two-hundred-rupee sari, a big bindi, a mangalsutra and glass bangles. I transformed myself into a *bharatiya nari*, the stereotypical traditional

Indian woman, and took my father along with me to meet the devadasis.

This time, when we went there, upon seeing my aged father, they said, 'Namaste.'

My father introduced me. 'This is my daughter and she is a teacher. She has come here on a holiday. I told her how difficult your lives are. Your children are the reason for your existence and you want to educate them irrespective of what happens to your health, am I right?'

They replied in unison, 'Yes, sir!'

'Since my daughter is a teacher, she can guide you with your children's education and help them find better jobs. She'll give you information about some scholarships which you may not be aware of and help your kids apply so that your financial burden may be reduced. Is that okay with you? If not, it's all right. She'll go to some other village and try to help the people there. Please don't feel pressured. Think about it and get back to us. We'll be back in ten minutes.'

Grasping my hand tightly, he pulled me a short distance away.

'Why did you say all that?' I asked. 'You should have first told them about things like the dangers of AIDS.'

'Don't be foolish. We will tell them about it some other time. If you start with something negative, then nobody will like it. The first introduction should always be positive and bring real hope to the beneficiary. And just like I've promised them, you must help their children get scholarships first. Work on AIDS later.'

'And why did you tell them I'm a teacher, Kaka?' I demanded. 'You could have said I was a social worker.'

My father offered a calm rebuttal. 'They consider teaching to be one of the most respectable jobs and you are a professor, aren't you?'

I nodded reluctantly, still unsure of his strategy.

When we went back, the women were ready to listen. They called me 'akka'.

So I started working with them to help their children secure the promised scholarships. Some of these children even started going to college within a year. Only after this happened did I bring up the subject of AIDS, and this time, they heard me out. Months went by. It took me almost three years to establish a relationship with them. I was their darling akka and eventually, they trusted me enough to share their heart-rending stories and the trials they had endured.

Innocent girls had been sold into the trade by their husbands, brothers, fathers, boyfriends, uncles or other relatives. Some entered the sex trade on their own, hoping to earn some money for their families and help future generations escape poverty. Still others were lured into it with the promise of a real job, only to find themselves tricked into sex work. Hearing their stories, there were moments when I couldn't hide my tears, yet they were the ones who held my hand and consoled me! Each story was different but the end was the same—they all suffered at the hands of a society that exploited them and filled them with guilt and shame as a final insult.

I realized that simply donating money would not bolster their confidence or build their self-esteem. The best solution I could think of was to unite them towards a common goal by helping them build their own organization. The state government of Karnataka had many good policies that encouraged housing, marriage schemes and scholarships, but if we started an association or a union exclusively for the devadasis, they could address each other's problems. In time, they would become bold and independent, learning to organize themselves in the process.

Thus, an organization for the devadasis was formed. I believe that God cannot be present everywhere at once and, instead, he sends people to do his work. Abhay Kumar, a kind-hearted and idealistic young man from Delhi, joined us unexpectedly. He wanted to work with me and so I decided to give him the toughest job in order to test his passion for social work. I told Abhay, 'If you work with the devadasis for eight months and survive, I'll think about absorbing you into the project full-time.'

As promised, he did not show up for eight months, and then one day, he confidently strolled into my office, a little thinner, but grinning from ear to ear.

I said, 'Abhay, now you know how hard social work is. It takes extreme commitment and persistence to keep going.

'You can go back to Delhi with the satisfaction of having made a difference to so many lives. You are a good human being and I'm sure that this little experience will stay with you and help you later.'

He smiled and replied in impeccable Kannada, 'Who said that I wanted to go back to Delhi? I've decided to stay in Karnataka and complete this project.'

'Abhay, this is serious work. You are young and that's a great disadvantage in this line of work and . . .' My voice faded away. I didn't know what else to say!

'Don't worry about that, madam! You gave me the best job I could possibly have. I thought that you might give me a desk job. I never imagined that you'd give me fieldwork, that too the privilege of working with the devadasis. This past year has made me realize their agony and unbearable hardships. Knowing that, how can I ever work anywhere apart from here?'

I was astonished at such sincerity and compassion in one so young. I offered him a stipend to help with his expenses but he stopped me with a show of his hand, 'I don't need that much. I already have a scooter and a few sets of clothes. I just need two meals a day, a roof over my head and a little money for petrol. That's it.'

I gazed at him fondly and knew that I was seeing a man who had found his purpose in life. He bade goodbye and left my office with determined strides.

Obviously, Abhay became the project lead, and I supported him wholeheartedly, taking care to converse with him regularly about the project's progress.

One day, I met with the devadasis and inquired about the welfare of their children.

'Our greatest difficulty is supporting our children's education,' they said. 'Most of the time, we can't afford their school fees and then we have to go back to what we know to get quick money.'

'We will take care of all your children's educational expenses, irrespective of which class they are in. But that means that you must not continue being a devadasi, no matter what,' I replied firmly.

The women agreed without hesitation. They had come to trust Abhay and me and knew that we would keep our word.

Hundreds of children were enrolled in the project—some went on to do professional courses while others went on to complete their primary-, middle- or high-school classes.

We held camps on AIDS awareness and prevention and sponsored street art and plays to educate the women and children on various medical issues—including the simple fact that infected hair is not an indication that one must become a devadasi. Rather, it is a simple curable disease that causes the hair to stick together and become matted over time. The women got themselves treated and some of them even had their heads shaved.

Eventually, we were able to get them loans by becoming their guarantors. Often, the women would tell me, 'Akka, please help us get a loan. If we can't repay it, then it is as good as cheating you and you know that we'll never do that.'

By this time I knew in my heart that a rich man might cheat me but our devadasis never would. They had great faith in me and I in them.

On the other hand, life became more dangerous for Abhay and me. We received death threats from pimps, local goons and others through phone calls, letters and messages. I was scared more for Abhay than myself. Though I asked for police protection, Abhay flatly refused and said, 'Our devadasis will protect me. Don't worry about me.'

A few weeks later, some pimps threw acid on three devadasis who had left their profession for good. But we all still refused to give up. The plastic surgery the victims underwent helped to bring back their confidence. They would not be intimidated. Our strength came from these women who were collectively trying to leave this hated profession. Though the government supplemented their income, many also started rearing goats, cows and buffaloes.

Over time, we established small schools that offered night classes which the devadasis could attend. It was an uphill battle that took years of effort from everybody involved.

After twelve years, some of the women met me to discuss a particular issue.

'Akka, we want to start a bank, but we are afraid to do it on our own.'

'What do you think happens in a bank?' I asked.

'Well, you need a lot of money to start a bank or even have an account. You must wear expensive clothes. We've seen that bankers usually wear suits and ties and sit in air-conditioned offices, but we don't have money for such things, Akka.'

After they brought this problem to our attention, Abhay and I sat down with the women and explained the basics of banking to them. A few professionals were consulted, and under their guidance, they started a bank of their own, with the exception of a few legal and administrative services that we provided. However, we insisted that the bank employees and shareholders should be restricted only to the devadasi community. So finally, the women were able to save money through fixed deposits and obtain low-interest loans. All profits had to be shared with the bank members. Eventually, the bank grew and the women themselves became its directors and took over its running.

Less than three years later, the bank had Rs 80 lakh in deposits and provided employment to former devadasis, but its most important achievement was that almost 3000 women were out of the devadasi system.

On their third anniversary, I received a letter from the bank.

We are very happy to share that three years have passed since the bank was started. Now, the bank is of sound financial health and none of us practise or make any money through the devadasi tradition. We have each paid a hundred rupees and have three lakhs saved for a big celebration. We have rented out a hall and arranged lunch for everyone. Please come and join us for our big day. Akka, you are very dear to us and we want you to be our chief guest for the occasion. You have travelled hundreds of times at your own cost and spent endless money for our sake even though we are strangers. This time, we want to book a round-trip air-conditioned Volvo bus ticket, a good hotel and an all-expenses-paid trip for you. Our money has been earned legally, ethically and morally. We are sure that you won't refuse our humble and earnest request.

Tears welled up in my eyes. Seventeen years ago, chappals were my reward, but now, they wanted to pay for my travel to the best of their ability. I knew how much the comfort of an air-conditioned Volvo bus and a hotel meant to them.

I decided to attend the function at my expense.

On the day of the function, I found that there were no politicians or garlands or long speeches as was typical. It was a simple event. At first, some women sang a song of agony written by the devadasis. Then another group came and described their experiences on their journey to independence. Their children, many of whom had become doctors, nurses, lawyers, clerks, government employees, teachers, railway employees and bank officers came and thanked their mothers and the organization for supporting their education.

And then it was my turn to speak.

I stood there, and words suddenly failed me. My mind went blank, and then, distantly, I remembered my father's words: 'I will feel very proud knowing that I gave birth to a daughter who helped ten helpless women make the most difficult transition from being sex workers to independent women.'

I am usually a spontaneous speaker but on that day, I was too choked with emotion. I didn't know where to begin. For the first time in my life, I felt that the day I meet God, I will be able to stand up straight and say confidently, 'You've given me a lot in this lifetime, and I hope that I have returned at least something. I've served 3000 of your children in the best way I could, relieving them of the meaningless and cruel devadasi system. Your children are your flowers and I am returning them to you.'

Then my eyes fell on the women. They were so eager to listen to me. They wanted to hear what I had to say. Abhay was there too, looking overwhelmed by everything they had done for us.

I quoted a Sanskrit sloka my grandfather had taught me when I was six years old: 'O God, I don't need a kingdom nor do I desire to be an emperor. I don't want rebirth or the golden vessels or heaven. I don't need anything from you. O Lord, if you want to give me something, then give me a soft heart and hard hands, so that I can wipe the tears of others.'

Silently, I came back to my chair. I didn't know what the women must be thinking or feeling at that moment.

An old devadasi climbed up on to the stage and stood there proudly. With a firm voice, she said, 'We want to give our akka a special gift. It is an embroidered bedspread and each of us has stitched some portion of it. So there are three thousand stitches. It may not look beautiful but we all wanted to be present in this bedspread.' Then she looked straight at me and continued, 'This is from our hearts to yours. This will keep you cool in the summer and warm in the winter—just like our affection towards you. You were by our side during our difficult times, and we want to be with you too.'

It is the best gift I have ever received.

22

The Meaning of Philanthropy

One day, I attended a wedding in the family and met my friends and relatives after a long time. Since we were guests and not part of the organizing committee, there was plenty of time for us to chat. Everybody was giving updates about their lives as we sat in a group when the conversation moved to the topic of giving back to our country and society.

One of the women opined, 'Philanthropy needs a lot of time. Also, a woman must be financially strong and have fewer responsibilities at home. Assuming that there are no other hobbies that she is passionate about, it is possible to pay attention to charitable work.'

'I think it is all to do with unpaid debts,' remarked a cousin. 'If a person has taken assistance from someone in a previous lifetime and they haven't repaid that debt, be it financially or physically, then the person must repay the debt in this lifetime. So, all it means is that philanthropists have taken a lot of help in their last birth and are simply repaying those debts now.'

Another woman said, 'You don't need talent when it comes to distributing money for charity. It is nothing but a way to pass time.' Then she looked at me with a friendly smile and asked, 'You are from the industry. What do you think?'

I knew that the intentions of my family and friends weren't bad at all. So, I did not get hurt or feel upset. With time, I have become insensitive to unhelpful comments and more sensitive to causes. I explained to them as best as I could. 'In my long journey of philanthropy,' I said, 'I have met many people who have helped others, irrespective of their circumstances. For instance, some of them did not have any money, some had a little, while there were others who had more than they would ever need. The only thing you really need to be a philanthropist is the attitude and determination to assist others.'

'Give me an example,' said one of them.

'Of course I will. That is the best way to convince you. You must have travelled at least once from the Badami railway station to the town. There are huge neem trees on either side of the road. The story goes that there once lived a lame man who wanted to make a difference. So, he planted neem saplings all by himself on both sides of the road. In the old days, there was sufficient rain and not much global warming. So the plants grew into trees. Today, however, no one remembers his name and all that remains is a story of an unknown lame man who provided shade to all the future travellers on that road. Tell me, isn't that an act of charity?'

There were 'oohs' and 'aahs' from the women sitting around me.

'Tell us more,' a few chorused. I noticed more people joining our group.

'Well, there is a well-known urologist in Bangalore named Dr Sridhar. He lived and worked abroad before making a decision to come back to the country. He could easily have decided otherwise and worked for a private hospital in a foreign land and earned much more money. Instead this doctor lives with his family in a two-bedroom rented home for the last thirty-one years and works every day towards fulfilling his dream of providing a professional opinion and helping people, with complete disregard to financial consideration. He has found a way to do this by making a clear demarcation in the way he works. He sees patients in the morning and charges his usual fees. However, in the evening, between 4 p.m. and 6 p.m., he sees each patient for free, irrespective of the income of the patients. Thus, he balances both parts of his life with sincerity.

'When I asked him the secret behind his noble deed, he said, "I have a very understanding and supportive wife and encouraging children, who have allowed me to go down this road. I wouldn't have been able to do so without them." That's when it hit me that even in philanthropy, great things cannot be achieved without family support.'

I saw a few nods in the group.

I continued. 'Recently, I was in Jaipur for work. While I was travelling in the city, my driver stopped to go to a dhaba and have tea. While waiting, I saw a beautiful farm surrounded by a boundary wall. There was a patch of green vegetables between the boundary wall and the road, and I saw a gardener working there. Curious, I went up to him and started a conversation. "Why are you working outside the boundary? Who does this patch belong to?" Just then, a big and strong man came out of the farm and headed towards the patch. When I asked him the same question, he invited me to come inside and have a look. I went in and immediately realized that the land belonged to a rich family. When I threw some more questions at the man, he said, "This is my ancestral land. I realize deeply that there are others who do not have land and are not as fortunate as I am. So, I decided to grow a few simple vegetables like coriander, spinach, fenugreek and other green leafy ones in the patch outside. The gardener has been instructed to take care of it in the same way that he takes care of the rest of my land. I have also told him to let anyone take the vegetables from there without question. He must only do his work with sincerity."

'I was surprised. "Who takes the vegetables?" I asked.

"There are many labourers who work around here. They come and pick some up."

"What happens if a person who isn't poor takes it?"

"Then I feel nothing but pity for him or her, but we don't say anything. I have been doing this for many years now, and everyone in this area knows that poor people get free vegetables from this garden." I was amazed at his quiet benevolence.'

I looked around and saw everyone listening with rapt attention. A cousin smiled and asked me to continue with a show of her hand.

'Let me tell you of another incident. In Rajasthan, people believe that giving free water to people is a pious act, especially in the summer. I saw mud pots on the side of the road that were almost always filled with water for passers-by. One day,

I saw a man taking away the mud pot. Unable to contain my inquisitiveness, I asked him, "Why are you carrying this? This must always be kept filled and on the side of the road."

'The man gave me a slight smile. He said, "Behenji, people happily fill water in the pots, but what they fail to realize is that the same pot can become a source of infectious diseases if nobody cares to clean it. So, once the pot is empty, my job is to thoroughly clean it and only then fill it with drinking water."'

'Ah!' The crowd around me chorused.

A friend remarked, 'I know many autorickshaw drivers in the city who drive old and sick people and pregnant women free of charge once a week.'

'Yes, that's exactly what philanthropy is about. Philanthropy is a Greek word where *philos* means loving and *anthropos* means man. Just like the autorickshaw drivers, the people I spoke about were not rich. Some were middle-class and some were poor. So, it isn't about how much a person has but their attitude towards fellow beings. It is compassion, a kind word, a warm hug and a little sharing that makes us better human beings. If we are lucky enough to be rich, then we can help more people. If a person can be a leader with compassion and a good attitude, then he or she can make a definite change in society. Don't you think?'

A murmur of agreement and hopeful sighs went through the group, even as someone announced that it was time for us to head to the next room for the wedding meal. Quickly, the group split into smaller clusters as we headed towards some well-deserved lunch.